THE
PAPER
CELL

CONTRABAND POCKET CRIME COLLECTION

THE PAPER CELL

Louise Hutcheson

CONTRABAND

CONTRABAND

An imprint of Saraband,
Digital World Centre, 1 Lowry Plaza
The Quays, Salford, M50 3UB
www.saraband.net

ISBN: 9781910192832
ISBNe: 9781910192955

10 9 8 7 6 5 4 3 2 1

Printed and bound in the EU
on paper from sustainable sources.

Louise Hutcheson has a PhD
in Scottish Literature from
the University of Glasgow.
She is a freelance editor of fiction,
and this is her first book.

The Paper Cell is the first in an occasional
series of quality crime novellas:
the Contraband Pocket Crime Collection.

Prologue

London, 1953

Two days before her death, Fran Watson paid him a visit at the office of Hobbs publishing house in Peckham.

The hemline of her brown skirt had dropped, and she picked at its frayed edges with nails that were raw and bitten. Her hair had frizzed in the humid air outside, and her plain, freckled face was glum.

She looked up only briefly before returning her gaze to her too-old skirt.

Lewis shifted behind his desk, aiming to look uncomfortable and achieving it. He affected a grimace as her eyes flitted up, then down. It was a pleasing dynamic, he thought. Though she had arrived when he was at the height of a bad temper, her obvious defects made him feel rather good about himself by comparison. He became aware of his finger tapping merrily on the desk and stilled himself. She had asked him a question, but he had not answered, deciding that his deliberate silence was eloquent enough in itself.

Finally, she nodded. 'I see. Well, you've been very candid, Mr Carson.' She stood abruptly, pushing aside a strand of hair that had escaped from behind her ear. 'Thank you for your time. I'll see myself out.'

'Miss Watson.' She paused in the doorway. 'Thank you

for approaching Hobbs. We do hope you find a more suitable publisher for your story.' A barely-there emphasis on that last word.

Lewis experienced a moment of deep satisfaction as she slammed the door. He sat for a while, enjoying the quiet. Eventually his gaze fell upon the manuscript, still sitting in the middle of the desk.

Infinite Eden
by F. Watson

He had not even read it. That is how cruel he was. But for the next two hours, he pored over its pages – once, twice, three times – returning compulsively again and again to the first page with a growing sense of horror.

The editorial team left the offices at seven, but he remained at his desk. At 9.47pm, he switched on the desk lamp and read the manuscript one last time.

He thought about her thick ankles and the dull sheen of sweat on her upper lip, the threadbare patches on her cardigan and how the clasp on her bag didn't latch properly. *Shit.* She was brilliant. Her work was brilliant.

Two days later, on a warm Wednesday morning, they would find her body in some shrubbery on Peckham Rye Common. She had been strangled.

I

Edinburgh, 1998

It seemed sudden at the time, but looking back, he realised that the end of his career had crept up insidiously. Throughout his life, he had enjoyed plotting out the narrative of his success by assigning significance to small events, meetings, choices such as these. Later, he couldn't help but do the same for his failures. He thought it might have begun on the day he met the journalist.

It was 1998, and he was sixty-seven years old.

In the library on George IV Bridge, Lewis fingered the spine of the book, admiring the series of cracks that ran its length, and eased it off the shelf. The last date stamp read '12 June, 1998', which prompted a smile. *Caroline*, his third novel, still being read by –

He paused to take stock of his fellow library patrons. An old woman, bent almost to the waist, reading the daily papers with her hat and anorak still on. Two students browsing the travel section. A bored clerk. The clerk glanced up at him, and Lewis slid the book back onto the shelf.

He worried for a moment that his more recent novels were absent before comforting himself with the thought that they were out on loan. His gaze was drawn to a free-standing display, on which someone had stuck a 'Scottish

Fiction' sign onto a large, crudely painted Saltire flag. This caused him to smirk, but he decided it was better than a thistle. He sighed when he saw that they had placed a second edition of *Caroline* next to Kelman's Booker-winning novel. Taped to the shelf below the books was a card that read simply 'controversial literature'.

The silence of the library was broken as a troop of toddlers marched hand-in-hand through the front doors, shepherded by three young women wearing matching yellow t-shirts. A nursery outing, he presumed. The clerk sighed as the chain of children broke apart, running in various directions, their excited voices pitched at a level that would have earned him and his classmates a cuff on the ear, back in the day. *Back in the day,* he scolded himself. How clichéd. The old woman pulled her trolley tight against her hip as if afraid one of the children would make off with it. She shook her head and sought his eye, seeking an ally. He did not want to be complicit, and instead turned a brief smile towards one of the young chaperones, who ignored him. Chastened, he turned his attention back the main fiction shelf.

On the left of *Caroline* was a sorry-looking edition of Camus' *The Stranger*. It wasn't bad company to keep, he supposed. On its right was – fuck. *Victory Lap* by Lewis Carson, unnoticed in his first scan of the shelf. He snatched the book from its place and rifled through its pages. It was the 1974 twentieth anniversary edition, a black-and-white photograph of his own face smiling out from the cover flap. He thumbed to the back and read the blurb.

In 1950s London, the young widow of a disgraced soldier struggles with sexual, political and social exclusion. A tragic meditation on post-war attitudes towards love and heroism, Victory Lap *has established itself as one of the classics of the twentieth century. This beautiful anniversary edition features a new foreword by the author and an introduction by James O'Hare.*

'Uncompromising and elegant in its execution, devastating in its impact.' THE TIMES

The book felt heavy as he replaced it on the shelf. It had been – what? – ten, fifteen years since he last held a copy in his hand. He leaned against the shelving and ran fingers through thin hair. Moisture broke above his lip, and a sense of compulsive, intense distaste filled his mouth.

'Dad?'

His gaze swung upwards to where his daughter's concerned face hovered. She deposited her own stack of books onto the carpet and placed a hand across his brow.

'Don't fuss,' he muttered, waving her away. 'I was just feeling a bit warm.'

A glance at her face told him she didn't believe him. She had spotted the pretty edition of *Victory Lap*, not quite flush with the rest of the books on the shelf. She pursed her lips and nudged it back in place.

'Perhaps we should rearrange with Barbara. Get you back home?'

He waved a hand dismissively and bent down to retrieve her books. An Indian cookbook, two antiques guides and a crime novel. 'Don't be daft. I was only tired.'

She merely shrugged and steered him towards the clerk, who had been watching his episode with open curiosity.

'Are you sure you're alright?' Sarah pressed. The clerk continued to eye him as she stamped Sarah's books, her mouth an ignorant-looking small 'o' amongst otherwise flat, dull features. Lewis glowered back at her, his annoyance only intensified by Sarah's tutting at his elbow.

'Yes, yes, please stop fussing.' He shook her hand off his elbow, which provoked a raised eyebrow from the clerk. Sarah caught her eye, and they both sighed.

'Artistic temperament,' she smiled, a joke at his expense.

The clerk nodded, as though she knew all too well. Lewis's patience for it all had long since dissipated. When finally it was finished, he moved towards the exit with an old man's relief.

The journalist was already waiting in the café when they arrived. She was perhaps forty, all bright prints and clattering plastic jewellery as she stood to shake his hand. Her hair was a brassy blonde, a bright, fluffy halo framing a round, cheerful face. He instantly disliked her.

'Mr Carson. I'm Barbara.' She had a limp grip but compensated by bringing her left hand up to clasp his palm between her two. It was a curiously intimate gesture, and he was glad when she released him.

Sarah moved to slide his jacket from his shoulders but he shrugged her off. She either didn't care or didn't realise he was aware of her eye-rolling – an unattractive, smug habit he wished she would cease – but she at least allowed him to settle himself. Barbara eyed them as Sarah ascertained he would like a black coffee, no sugar, her gaze drinking in what he thought was a fairly standard exchange.

'Please call me Lewis,' he said, offering a smile.

Barbara nodded cheerfully. She waited until Sarah had disappeared to the counter before pulling a dictaphone out of a pink leather handbag. She raised an eyebrow in his direction, a silent query of consent. He nodded.

'I'm so pleased to finally meet you, Lewis. Really.'

He didn't respond. She cleared her throat, and he enjoyed a moment of strained silence.

'Yes. So, as I mentioned in our emails, our chat today will form the bulk of a 2,000-word feature on you for this Sunday's Arts page. Any questions before we start, or shall I crack on?' She smiled brightly, her briskness and efficiency at odds with her jamboree appearance.

Lewis nodded his assent, his eyes fixed on the oversized roses that dotted her cheap blouse. She cleared her throat again and adjusted the blouse's neckline. She thought he was staring at her chest, he realised. He smiled at her, pleased by the pink flush in her cheeks. He had no interest in her pendulous breasts, but that she was discomfited satisfied his sudden urge to wrong-foot her.

'The piece will be a complete retrospective.' She ducked her head to catch his eye. He waited a beat before pulling his gaze up to meet hers. Her cheeks remained pink, and he saw her self-consciously pluck at the deep V-line of the blouse once more.

'Prompted by what?' he asked, steepling his fingers under his chin.

'Prompted?' she parroted back, nonplussed.

'A retrospective is usually prompted by a milestone in one's career. Or by one's death. Neither apply in my case,' he said.

Her expression cleared. 'This is the first interview you've agreed to for over eleven years,' she said, smiling. 'And as you're not just peddling your latest publication—' at this she jostled his elbow, as though she had made some excellent joke, 'it seemed an obvious approach.'

Satisfied with herself, she switched on the dictaphone and placed it carefully on the table between them. She lined up her coffee cup and saucer, sat back and surveyed their setup with a smile. She reminded him of a toddler, he realised, stacking her bright bricks and quite convinced of her own cleverness.

'You haven't been writing for the paper for very long, have you?' he asked, though he wasn't at all interested in her career.

She looked up to catch his eye, unsure if his tone suggested something she ought to be offended by. He smiled at her, and she tapped the recorder with a long, painted nail, still unsure.

'No, not for the *Herald*.' She pulled her shoulders back, asserting herself. He deliberately dropped his gaze back down to her neckline. 'But I was on the features desk of the *Evening Times* for seven years prior to that,' she said, her hand fluttering to her cleavage. He smiled.

'I thought we'd start by talking about Ann Barbour,' she said then, catching him off guard.

'About Ann?' he repeated, rattled. His eyes refocused on her face, and she smiled sweetly. It occurred to him that she was sharper than he had given her credit for.

'Why would you want to discuss Mum?' Sarah interjected, having appeared at his elbow with two steaming cups and a large slab of cake.

Barbara's brow creased, irritated by her reappearance. She directed her response to Lewis, ignoring his daughter. He was quite certain Sarah had just rolled her eyes again.

'Your ex-wife recently spoke to an arts website about her early career, as well as yours,' she said. There was something like a hungry gleam in her eye, and Lewis felt himself tense. 'She spoke quite candidly about your relationship at that time.'

Lewis swallowed. 'I haven't had the pleasure of reading it.'

Sarah snorted into her coffee mug. She took a sip and clattered the mug down on the table, sloshing mahogany liquid precariously close to the recorder. Barbara reached out and adjusted its placement.

'I've read it,' Sarah said, levelling her gaze at Barbara. 'Mum gets confused sometimes, you know. People put words in her mouth and she agrees with it because she's not sure if they're right or not.'

'It was a very good, insightful article,' Barbara responded, not at all cowed.

'Yes, well truth and good reading don't necessarily go hand in hand,' Lewis said.

Sarah nodded and folded her arms across her body. She was upset, he realised.

'Ann was diagnosed with early-onset dementia some years ago,' he said, patting Sarah's knee as he did so.

She looked down at his hand.

Barbara flushed. 'There were rumours, of course,' she said, flashing what might have been an apologetic look in Sarah's direction.

Sarah sniffed and shifted her leg so that Lewis's hand fell away. She would not be his ally in this, he thought.

'I haven't read Ann's article and I don't care to discuss it, or her,' he said.

Barbara pursed her lips, and to his left, Sarah relaxed her pose.

'Of course.' Barbara's head bobbed. She tapped her fingernail against the edge of the recorder, regrouping her thoughts. She looked briefly at a set of scribbled notes and nodded to herself.

The atmosphere was heavy – hostile, even, as the silence between them lengthened. It was episodes like this that had earned Lewis a reputation amongst journalists. Being a notoriously difficult interview subject wasn't an image he liked to cultivate, and he was annoyed that she had so quickly fallen into the same pattern as her predecessors. He remained very still, wishing to break the silence but unsure how to do so. When he eventually reached out to take a sip of his coffee, Barbara seemed to rally herself.

'Let's move on,' she said, fixing a smile to her face. 'We'll start at the logical place – your first novel.'

Sarah stiffened visibly by his side. He set the coffee mug back on its saucer, despising the slight tremor in his hand. So much for their truce, he mused. It had lasted mere seconds.

'Dad doesn't discuss *Victory Lap* any more,' Sarah said. 'And I think you know that full well.'

Yes, he thought, *she's right*. Not for many years. And everyone knew. Everyone knew not to try, not to sour the atmosphere. 'Prickly' is how he'd been described by some; 'downright aggressive' by others who persisted with their questions. Everyone knew.

Barbara ignored Sarah's comment and instead stared at Lewis. A bead of moisture ran down the back of his neck. The steamed windows of the café suddenly seemed oppressive, and the smell of damp wool made his nostrils flare. A child wailed from a table nearby, throwing a teaspoon to the floor with a clatter.

'Come on, Lewis – let's be blunt. *Something* made you accept my interview request. Something made you break a decade's silence. This was never going to be *just another interview*. What did you expect? Another banal, respectful puff piece that skirts carefully around your temper? It's not what I came for, and I suspect it's not what you want either.'

He stared back at her, unprepared for her candidness.

'You were briefed on this. What did *you* expect?' Sarah's voice was hard, and Barbara tutted.

It was too much for Sarah. She leaned across the table, her finger raised, about to jab against Barbara's breastbone. Lewis grabbed her hand, his breath shallow, and moved to stand. He was disgusted when his knee trembled and gave out beneath him. He lurched back into the chair.

'Dad,' Sarah said, leaping forward to support his arm.

'I don't...' His breath huffed out, constricted, and he patted at his chest.

'Dad, are you all right? Dad? Dad?' Sarah came to kneel in front of him, her eyes darting between him and the barista at the counter, who was staring stupidly, a shaker with cinnamon dusting on its head hanging forgotten in his hand.

'Call an ambulance!' Sarah ordered.

He was wheezing – too hot, too tight to breathe. He patted his chest and felt his eyes roll upwards towards the ceiling.

'Can I help?' Barbara's round face hovered above him, a vague blonde haze, her facial features blurring into a bland, sallow melt. She squeezed his shoulder.

'Leave him,' Sarah spat.

He couldn't see her any more, his head lolling on the back of the chair and his eyes gazing near-sightlessly up at Barbara's hazy features.

'I can't breathe,' he whispered, and Barbara's face mercifully disappeared into darkness.

London, 1953

Frederick Hobbs leant back in his chair and draped one slim ankle over the other, a pair of snow-white socks appearing in the gap between leather shoe and brown trouser leg. He assessed Lewis over the rim of thin, gold spectacles. Lewis met his gaze levelly.

'Remind me where you completed your degree, Lewis?'

'Edinburgh University, sir. English and History.'

Hobbs nodded and glanced back at the paperwork in his left hand. Lewis was almost certain it was the enquiry letter he had submitted to the publishing house last year, two months after he had graduated and moved to London. Frederick Hobbs II – great-grandson of Lawrence Hobbs (founder of Hobbs Books), not yet thirty years old, heir to the Hobbs fortune and a pompous shit who'd failed out of Cambridge before Daddy stepped in and gave him a job in the family business – was casting a dismissive eye over Lewis's greatest achievements. Lewis shifted uncomfortably in his seat, a move he regretted when Hobbs cast him a bemused glance. He stilled, reassuring himself that what Hobbs read was impressive. First Class degree, editor-in-chief of *The Student* newspaper for two years, a handful of essays published across minor magazines and journals.

That he was working at Hobbs at all was proof, he assured himself, that the move to London had been successful. Before he left Edinburgh, he had been working in the Post Office with his sister, sorting letters and selling stamps to a clientele comprising mostly of older women and smartly dressed secretaries who clacked in on stylish heels and stared at the ink stains on his fingers. Worst had been the days on which former classmates entered, or the true hell – Nathan Cochran's infernal mother, forever coming in to boast about her son's books, flashing clippings under everyone's nose of even the most mildly positive reviews. Lewis had read his classmate's novels: cheap, pulpy things with ridiculous *femme fatales* and a boring, by-the-numbers alcoholic detective. It disappointed him that Nathan represented the most successful of his peers. If it couldn't be him, it should at least have been someone more daring, more elegant. *Crime fiction.* He sighed.

Hobbs dropped the papers back on the desk and clasped his hands in his lap. 'My father feels that we are wasting you, Lewis, downstairs in accounts. Thinks you belong on this floor, assisting myself and the editorial team.'

Lewis felt his pulse quicken and his shoulders made an involuntary thrust towards Hobbs. 'Sir, I would be delighted, you have no idea how much I've –'

'Hold your horses, Carson. I didn't say I agreed.'

Lewis leant back, cursing his keenness as Hobbs smirked at him.

'I'm happy to have you up here, certainly. We sorely need some administrative assistance – taking the minutes for our editorial meetings, filing submissions and whatnot. More importantly, we don't have time to field all the drop-ins we've been receiving lately. Unless they come accompanied by a respected agent, we won't see them, so it will be up to you to politely show them out the door and in the direction of a more appropriate publisher. You will be our editorial assistant, of sorts.' Hobbs had dropped his gaze and was examining his fingernails. A pause, lengthy and deliberate, stretched between them. Finally, his eyes flitted briefly upwards. 'Does this appeal to you, Mr Carson?'

Lewis forced himself to pause before answering. His attempt to match Hobbs' calculated silence lasted a fraction of the time. It was not *strictly* the commissioning editor's role he had applied for last year. But...*a promotion*. His sister would tell Mrs Cochran over the post counter, relishing his victory for him even if she'd never understood the depths of his distaste for Nathan Cochran's bloated, brilliant inspector.

'Thank you, sir,' he said. 'I appreciate the opportunity.'

That evening, he telephoned Cathy from the pub across the road, and she burst into tears. 'A *commissioning* editor, Lewis? Oh, that is so wonderful!'

Edinburgh, 1998

'He's a compulsive liar.'

Lewis fixed his daughter with a deadly stare, and the paramedic laughed. 'Is that so, Mr Carson?' she grinned up at him from her kneeling position on the floor.

He had come round not moments after fainting, horrified by the gaggle of concerned onlookers in the busy café. Barbara had hovered at the edge of the proceedings, and he noted that her dictaphone continued to record from the table. When the barista came over to ask how he was, she overrode Sarah with a wave of her hand and announced in a carrying voice that he had suffered a mild panic attack. She wasn't wrong, but he longed for her to leave, or at the very least shut up. Silly bitch.

'He's lying,' Sarah insisted again, and his gaze returned to her. She stood behind the smiling paramedic, hands on hips and a harried air about her. Hair had sprung loose from her ponytail and she was flushed, agitated.

'I'm not lying,' he asserted.

'You didn't faint earlier this afternoon as well?' The paramedic attached a blood pressure monitor to his arm and pumped it up with brisk thrusts as she waited for his response.

Sarah arched an eyebrow at him.

'No,' he said.

Sarah threw her hands up in the air and stalked to the counter. The manager handed her a glass of water and patted her arm sympathetically.

'My daughter is being theatrical, as is her wont,' he said to the paramedic, his voice lowered.

The woman laughed again, and Sarah shot them a stern look over her shoulder. No matter.

'I took a turn in the library earlier. But I didn't faint.'

The paramedic looked to Sarah for confirmation. She nodded curtly, defeated, her cheeks pink.

'I've just been a bit warm today. It's been humid,' he added.

'All I was saying, Dad, is that you've been out of sorts all day. Obviously something's wrong,' said Sarah, her voice cutting across the café.

He huffed and looked at the heads swivelling between himself and his daughter.

The paramedic released the armband and rose to her feet. She seemed incredibly tall, and he had to crane his neck to meet her eye.

'Your blood pressure is a bit high,' she said, sounding unconcerned. Sarah opened her mouth to speak, and the paramedic held up a hand to stop her. 'But not so high as to cause alarm,' she added.

'I can go home then,' he said, pushing himself up from the chair. The paramedic pushed him down gently. He resisted the urge to swat her hands away.

'Not quite. A loss of consciousness twice in one afternoon – in a man of your age in particular – could suggest an underlying problem. I'd strongly advise you to accompany me to A&E for tests and observation,' she said.

'Once in an afternoon,' he corrected, loathing her.

'One loss of consciousness and a dizzy spell,' she conceded, and he was infuriated to see her throw a wink over her shoulder to Sarah. 'Either way, I'd ask you to come with me.'

'No,' he said, his tone final. The paramedic looked helplessly between Barbara and Sarah. He pushed himself to his feet, steady this time, and pulled his jacket around his shoulders.

Sarah's head drooped. She rubbed at her forehead. Barbara shrugged, an apologetic grimace on his behalf. *Stupid, idiotic woman.*

'Sarah, I'm going home,' he announced, pushing past the crowd of onlookers.

'*I think I know him from somewhere,*' a young man whispered to his girlfriend, and Lewis lengthened his gait.

Sarah caught up with him some five hundred yards along Lothian Road. The air was as humid as it had been earlier, but away from the stuffy café, the relative coolness soothed his moist forehead and swelled his lungs. They kept a brisk pace, Sarah primly silent, for which he was glad.

Now that he was outside, he felt hopelessly stupid.

He had come across the review for his last novel some three days prior, a newspaper clipping tucked behind an old electricity bill in his desk drawer.

'*Carson's sixth novel is as dazzling as his first, and I await his next with bated breath.*'

Thirteen years had passed since then. He hadn't written a single word in the interim. His last interview – before today's aborted effort – had taken place in the months after that publication, the last in a long series of repetitive sitdowns with eager journalists and one that had wearied him of the marketing cycle. He had stepped away, sold the townhouse in London and bought an end terrace in

Meadowside, close to Sarah and Ann.

But rediscovering that review – so obsequious, so thrilling – had sparked something in him he thought long dead. He wanted to be 'Lewis Carson, novelist', again. Not 'Lewis Carson, retired divorcee who potters around his compact garden and does the crossword puzzle on the terrace when it's warm enough.' So he had trawled through his recently deleted emails and spotted one from Barbara at the *Herald*.

Old fool, he thought. *Such pathetic vanity.*

'Why do you always do that?' Sarah asked, interrupting his mental self-flagellation.

'Do what?'

She sighed. 'You panic whenever your early career is mentioned. Ever since I was a girl. I grew up around your books, played in your office while you wrote, and even I don't know why you've so thoroughly distanced yourself from those years. Or from *Victory Lap*.'

He maintained his pace, though he felt his pulse flutter slightly. She had never asked him this before. Ann had; it was a constant needle, prick-prick-pricking at him until eventually he left. Sarah looped her arm through his, but kept silent. He contemplated for a moment what it would be like to tell her the truth. How her beloved father had become a celebrated writer, an award winner, a bestseller.

The silence stretched on.

'Never mind,' Sarah snapped eventually. She pulled her arm free and increased her pace, leaving him trailing behind her. He thrust his hands into his pockets and bowed his head, his thoughts locked on the past.

London, 1953

The editorial team were going for drinks, and Lewis had been invited.

They had collectively filed out of the office into a clammy spatter of rain, running across the street to the King's Head because it was the closest means of escape from such inclement weather. Lewis had ordered himself a pint and stood on the fringe of the group for the first half hour, too shy and too minor to be noticed. By the time he had drained the first glass he was feeling fairly superfluous and had considered leaving quietly before his presence became – god forbid – a silent nuisance. He'd have to get some chips on the walk home, maybe stretch as far as a fish supper. But then, why bother coming in the first place? Hadn't he hoped a conversation fuelled by beer and camaraderie might open some sort of confidence between himself and his colleagues? A stupid thought, he knew. But he had been nursing thoughts of intellectual bonding all afternoon, pulling out various copies of classic and modern poetry collections to refresh himself on their various styles, content and themes. Just in case. This rushed study had only served to further unnerve him, and he was now suffering from a searing sense of inferiority.

On top of this, Frederick Hobbs was pissing him off.

Since promoting him to the editorial floor (to a role Lewis had increasingly come to view as a glorified secretary), Hobbs had scrupulously and pointedly ignored his presence there. In the three months since Lewis had moved his books and notes up to the third floor, he had encountered Hobbs daily in the corridors. The only interaction they had shared thus far was an appreciative grunt from Hobbs during the course of delivering some paperwork. Lewis had handed him a series of copyright waivers, and for a brief second their thumbs had grazed. Hobbs darted a gaze at him above low-slung gold frames and looked oddly startled. Lewis attempted a smile, and Hobbs…grunted.

Tonight he had paid for and thrown back three whiskies in the time it had taken Lewis to drink a single pint. Hobbs was by no means behaving raucously, but was in fact standing at the end of the bar having an intense conversation with Simon More, the publishing house's senior poetry editor. Lewis was by this point fighting an internal battle with himself, partly enraged by this enduring public dismissal and partly exasperated that he even cared: Hobbs was a fraud, his role on the editorial board a product of cheap and obvious nepotism. Or so he had tried, with increasing desperation in recent months, to convince himself. He had sat in on enough editorial meetings now to have discerned Hobbs' surprising sense of taste and found himself struck by the innovative and exciting texts he brought to the table. It was an inconvenient reality with which he did daily battle.

He had wrestled with these feelings for weeks, often rehearsing conversations aloud in his flat in which he alternated between an imagined colloquium of great intellectual fervour and of simply embarrassing the smug bastard with his superior knowledge of, well, something. Either way, he was acutely aware of his growing preoccupation with Hobbs…and was uncomfortable with it.

Realising he wasn't yet willing to abandon the evening's cause, he deposited his empty pint glass on the bar and signalled to the landlord for a second serving. By the time the balding man had placed it in front of him and payment had been made, he was aware that a woman had stepped up beside him and intentionally jostled his elbow. He turned toward her.

'What's bothering you, Lewis? Not allowed to play with the big boys?' She inclined her head towards Hobbs, who was laughing at something More had said.

Lewis twisted rudely from her to face the bar again. Catching sight of her in the mirror, he saw she was far from perturbed.

'What makes you think that?' he finally offered.

Julie smiled as she lit a cigarette and leaned deliberately across the bar. She exhaled a large plume of smoke as she asked the landlord for a 'red wine – *not* merlot,' and waited until it had been presented to her before she answered.

'You've been burning holes into our dear leader all evening, sweetheart. Are you feeling left out? Well. He's obviously doing something to bring out the gruff Scot in you.' She paused to take an extravagantly long gulp of wine. 'Or is it something else? Low pay? Won't print your little story?'

Despite the patronising tone, he knew she was trying to flirt with him. She had a way of tucking her chin into her neck that she clearly thought was sultry but in fact only made her look chubby and gormless. She had also manoeuvred her elbows tight into her rib cage in an attempt to emphasise her breasts, which was working just fine. Nevertheless, he found her cheap and vulgar.

'I think you're two conspiracies shy of a pulp thriller, Julie,' he answered amiably enough, leaning back on the bar with his elbows so that he had to look at her from the side. 'Hobbs and I barely know one another.'

She shrugged her shoulders with emphasis and checked to see if he had appreciated the shift of her breasts as she did so. 'Whatever you say, Scotty.'

'Speaking of thrills –' He could tell she was trying to sound aloof. She paused for effect, her suggestion plain enough.

'We were? I thought we were speaking about your over-active imagination.'

She faltered, flustered, and he felt momentarily guilty.

'I only wondered if you were busy this evening,' she muttered, her face darkening as she ducked her nose into her drink. 'My flat…it's not far from here.'

She was clearly mortified. Lewis took a long drink from his glass. She had turned shy, gazing into her wine glass. She was an assistant in the fiction department, responsible primarily for proofing final copy. Though considered attractive by most of the publishing staff, she was by no means a great beauty. And no one important.

'Julie, I would love to. The thing is, I'm –'

'Seeing someone? Not interested?' she interrupted him, her cheeks dark and blotchy, and grabbed her handbag from the bar stool. 'No need to say any more, Lewis. I'll consider you a pal if you just forget this ever happened.'

With a final attempt at bravado, she sashayed to the door, wide hips swinging and head high. She got her consolation prize when Nicholas, a typesetter, abandoned a half-drunk pint and followed her onto the street.

Lewis finished his second pint and ordered another, then turned his attention back to Hobbs. A man with impeccable social graces, he flitted from group to group with ease. People watched him from across the room, hoping he would deign to speak to them next. Lewis watched as a blushing girl approached and touched his elbow, an encounter from which he politely extricated himself. It was a curious spectacle, the way people seemed to unconsciously cluster around him, and while Lewis feared that he'd be caught watching, he was unable to stop himself.

Hobbs' eyes lifted briefly in his direction, and he turned back to the bar too quickly. *Idiot.* He caught sight of his own reflection in the mirror and wondered for a moment what he looked like to an onlooker. He did not have Hobbs' elegance, that he knew. He wasn't quite as tall, and though lean, he felt that his fingers lacked length, his shoulders were not sharp enough. Where Hobbs was fair, his hair smoothed carefully off his forehead and cut with precision by an expensive barber, Lewis was dark. Strands of grey had begun to lighten the peak – surprisingly early, he felt – but he fancied it made him appear older and was actually quite fond of it. But he didn't interest anyone at the bar. People didn't watch him the way they did Hobbs. He was unremarkable. His expression in the mirror looked very serious.

Frowning at himself, he made a decision. With a fresh drink in hand, he joined Dickson and Goldstein at the far end of the bar, deliberately turning his back on Hobbs.

∗

Lewis was drunk. At some point in the evening, the eleven Hobbs staff had diminished to a mere four, including himself, and they had been buying rounds of whisky for some time. Lewis had run out of money at the last round and had rashly offered to have them back to the flat, where he had a decent bottle of the stuff anyway. Now they were walking along Peckham High Street towards his rented one bedroom studio apartment, and he was embarrassed already.

Frederick Hobbs was beside him, smelling strongly of spirits yet walking in a remarkably straight line. Lewis wanted to sober up and match his purposeful gait, but he was definitely ranging across the wet pavement.

'Julie not to your taste, then?' Hobbs suddenly piped up, arms tucked into ribs and hands in his pockets in an attempt to retain heat within his slim frame. Lewis was startled and found himself stopping in the street.

'She's horrid,' he answered, without thinking.

Hobbs barked a startled laugh and paused to appraise Lewis. Some minutes behind, Paul Goldstein and Alan Dickson had stopped to be violently sick in the gutter, one's projectile upwelling seeming to provoke the other's.

Lewis and Hobbs stood face to face, hands in pockets, appraising one another properly for the first time since that demeaning meeting in Hobbs' office three months prior.

Hobbs seemed to reach some sort of conclusion and nodded his head in the general direction of Lewis's flat. 'Let's batter on, then,' he said, before glancing back to Goldstein and Dickson's position down the street. 'I imagine your landlady would thank you to leave those two behind.'

Five minutes later, Hobbs was standing in front of the dresser in the flat, casually running his index finger over an oval frame of Lewis's parents on their wedding day. Lewis stood at the opposite side of the sitting room, holding two tumblers of whisky.

'You look like your father,' Hobbs said. Lewis ducked his head in acknowledgement and handed him the tumbler, the scent of peat and seaweed pleasant in the air.

'He's a Postmaster,' he finally said, sitting down on the sprung sofa. Hobbs looked politely interested but didn't offer a reply as he joined him.

The silence stretched companionably between them for a spell, in which they each took short sips of their drinks and ice danced merrily about Hobbs' glass. He had laughed as he asked for it, dismissing Lewis's raised eyebrow with, 'Purist, are we?'

'Poor Julie will be in a right strop,' Hobbs suddenly murmured, smiling faintly.

Lewis frowned into his tumbler, having entirely forgotten their encounter at the bar. 'I doubt she's heartbroken,' he replied.

'I don't know. She doesn't often make advances on the junior staff.' Hobbs was watching him from the corner of his eye.

Lewis uncrossed his legs and scratched at his jaw unnecessarily, wondering darkly if Julie had been talking about him. How embarrassing. He chose to ignore the casual condemnation of his status.

'She seems awfully taken with your accent,' Hobbs grinned.

It struck Lewis then that he was lying.

'Why did you drop out of Cambridge?' he asked, and Hobbs' smile vanished. A flush crept up his neck, and he shot Lewis a look of mock menace before answering.

'I can't decide if I'm offended or impressed by how rude that was.'

Lewis gazed pointedly back at him.

A sigh. 'I had a bit of a tiff with my Head of Department,' he offered, eventually.

'You dropped out of the most prestigious university in the country because you didn't fancy reading Yeats?'

'You're mocking me!'

'I'm sorry, I was joking. Was it Milton?'

Hobbs barked a quick laugh and looked down into his tumbler. Realising the truth was not forthcoming, Lewis shrugged and settled further down into the chair.

'I nearly dropped out of Edinburgh, you know,' he murmured.

Hobbs' raised eyebrow invited him to continue.

'My mother took very ill when I was in my second year. I thought about dropping out and going home to take care of her. She wouldn't let me. I stayed on to sit my exams, and she died alone in the house. Dad out at work, my sister at school.'

A vivid image of his mother appeared, unbidden, in his mind. Tall for a woman, wiry and lean with a sort of hard elegance, a deep blue skirt that reached her calves and a smatter of freckles between faint facial lines. She didn't work but occasionally took in the neighbours' sewing for a small fee. And she always smelled of the lavender talc Dad bought her for her birthdays and Christmases. She'd taught him and Cathy how to swim in the outdoor pool at Helensburgh, where their feet caught on jagged rocks and the water was salty.

Don't you dare come home, she'd said. *Don't you dare.*

'Lewis.'

'Sorry?' He returned to the room, disoriented.

'I have to – ugh, Christ. I'm sorry that I was unkind to you, the day I offered you the job on the third floor.' Hobbs took a rushed drink of whisky, leaving the ice to rattle against the glass rim. He stared into the now empty tumbler.

Lewis stood, prising the glass from Hobbs' elegant fingers, and crossed to the cabinet to refill it. His own fingers left a soft sheen of sweat on the whisky bottle, and he wiped his palm down his trouser leg.

'It's quite alright,' he said, his tone light.

'It's not. What must you have thought of me?' He stopped short at Lewis's fleeting smirk. 'That bad, eh?'

'I've spent many hours since plotting your very violent death.'

'Fuck off,' Hobbs laughed, looking delighted.

'Fuck you if you think it's funny. I've spent three months thinking about nothing other than ways to make you look at me differently.'

Hobbs had a serious expression on his face. 'How do you want me to look at you?'

'I don't know,' Lewis lied.

Hobbs was watching him. Lewis remembered himself and turned back to refill their tumblers. The ice had all but melted in his warm hands.

'I'll be back in a moment,' he said, brandishing the glasses in the air as explanation. He didn't look at Hobbs as he left the room.

The freezer was in the house basement, a luxury the landlady, Mrs Bell, was deeply proud of. Lewis loped down the three flights, dancing carefully around the creakier floorboards, aware that it was long past eleven and that Jenny Warren on the first floor would be sleeping already. She worked at the hospital in a role that required her to leave the boarding house at some ungodly hour. But as he reached the landing, her door was flung wide. Mrs Bell stared him down imperiously from the doorway, a glass of sherry in one hand and an angry-looking tabby cat draped across her arm.

He halted mid-stride, reflecting that she was at once the most striking and ridiculous woman he had ever seen. She must have been at least six feet tall, a trait she emphasised with imposingly high heels, and she was desperately lean. At one point in her life she might have been very beautiful. Lewis couldn't be sure of her precise age, but her tottering gait and deeply lined face suggested she was at the very least seventy years old. Her hair was vividly black and coiled in a thick, elegant spiral atop her head. She dripped with gold, and always wore a fat string of pearls around her neck.

'Lewis!' she said, beaming.

Jenny Warren gestured frantically from behind, her face a mask of misery. Lewis fought the urge to laugh. Jenny was a sweet girl – she hadn't yet learned that to live peacefully under Mrs Bell's roof, one must avoid Mrs Bell at all times.

'Mrs Bell,' he said, grinning. 'Miss Warren,' he added, nodding to an exasperated Jenny.

She continued to make inscrutable gestures behind Mrs Bell's back, and he squinted at her curiously.

'Have you been having a nice evening?' he asked them, and Jenny threw her hands in the air, clearly infuriated.

Mrs Bell crossed the hallway and extended her gaunt face in his direction. He knew that this was an invitation and kissed her politely on the cheek. She smelled of sweet sherry and floral perfume, and he drew back sharply. The cat had taken advantage of his closeness and hooked a claw in his shirt sleeve. Mrs Bell squawked as he pried it off.

'Pushkin has always been so fond of Lewis,' she told Jenny, smiling between the two lodgers.

Jenny nodded politely. 'Yes, yes. Goodnight now, Mrs Bell. I must be off to bed!'

She shut the door firmly, prompting Mrs Bell to quirk a quizzical brow. 'Awfully unsociable, that one. It's no wonder she's a spinster, really.'

Lewis was certain that Jenny would have heard Mrs Bell's stage whisper through her closed door and merely nodded.

'You know, you'd make a delightful couple,' she said, cackling. Pushkin, as perturbed by this outburst as Lewis was, leapt from her arms and made a dash for the upper floor. Mrs Bell looked unconcerned and looped her free arm through Lewis's.

'I'm sure Miss Warren has plenty of suitors.'

He sounded prim, he realised, and Mrs Bell snorted disbelievingly. She noted the two empty tumblers in his hand.

'You have a guest,' she said, unaccountably pleased. 'Is it a lady friend?'

He blanched, and she patted his hand.

'You and Miss Warren, such a private pair. It's no wonder you're both unmarried, I tell you. But you know, you'd make a delightful couple.'

He cleared his throat to avoid answering – it was a familiar refrain – but was spared their usual back-and-forth when a light tread on the stairwell behind him announced Hobbs' arrival.

'Oh, look there! Pushkin has found a new friend.' Mrs Bell peeled the cat from Hobbs' arms and planted a loud kiss on its head. The cat wriggled uncomfortably, and she bent down to release him. Lewis met Hobbs' eye over her stooped frame and shrugged apologetically.

'Mrs Bell, this is Frederick Hobbs. We were drinking with some colleagues this evening,' he added, aware that it might be unusual for him to have someone in his room so late.

Mrs Bell shooed him to the side and embraced Hobbs by the shoulders. Despite her height, he stood a head taller than her and looked down at her with some amusement. If he felt any distaste, Hobbs hid it well.

'A pleasure, Mrs Bell,' he said, clasping her hands between his own. She beamed at him, sherry stains and lipstick darkening her teeth.

Lewis felt the warmth of embarrassment, but Hobbs seemed unperturbed. She peered up at his face as though searching for some familiar feature.

'I know your grandfather, boy!' she declared, surprising them both.

'You do?' Hobbs asked, a fleeting look of scepticism swiftly replaced with a nod of polite interest.

'Oh, yes, we used to dine in the Cecil together, Mr Hobbs. I know him quite well, you know.' She leaned in. 'He tried to kiss me once, but I slapped his face!'

Laughter burst from Hobbs' lips, surprising Lewis.

'I don't doubt it, Mrs Bell,' Hobbs said, sweeping an arm around her back and guiding her up the stairwell. 'He always said he only courted the most beautiful young women.'

She simpered, delighted, and the two continued on towards Lewis's room.

'Lewis,' Hobbs said, looking over his shoulder with a sly wink. 'Bring up enough for Mrs Bell as well. I want to hear all about my grandfather's wild youth.'

Lewis watched them ascend, nonplussed. When they disappeared into his room, he turned to go downstairs. Jenny Warren opened her door a crack and peered out at him.

'If you could try to keep her quiet, I'd be very grateful,' she whispered. Lewis winked, and she closed the door silently.

✳

It was long gone one-thirty by the time Lewis was able to usher Mrs Bell out of his room and downstairs to her own living quarters. She occupied the ground floor of the house, and he and Hobbs had been forced to carry her down between the two of them.

'If he's anything like his grandfather,' she crowed mercilessly up the stairs as they retreated, 'he'll be up until the rooster sings!'

They smothered a laugh, and Hobbs hooked an arm around Lewis's shoulder as they made their way back up to the third floor. Lewis felt curiously sober, though Hobbs, he noticed, had lost his steady gait.

'I'm so sorry,' he whispered as he closed the door, gesturing down at the floor as though Mrs Bell might be lying at his feet, swilling cheap sherry and telling inappropriate stories about Lawrence Hobbs.

'She's so obscene!' Hobbs said, with a tone of delight. 'I can see why my grandfather would have liked her.'

'Quite,' Lewis replied, and they both sniggered.

Lewis was leaning against the closed door, Hobbs against the dresser at the opposite side of the room. A small silence bloomed, into which their smiles slowly faded.

'Where were we,' Hobbs mused, 'before the lovely Mrs Bell joined us?'

'Which she did at your invitation,' Lewis reminded him, his admonishing tone only half serious.

Hobbs smiled. 'She was an interesting distraction,' he replied, shrugging.

Once more, a small silence grew. Lewis studied Hobbs.

Even drunk, his eyes somewhat bleary, he was elegant. Tall and lean and neat, his fair hair smoothed off his face. Lewis self-consciously touched his own hair. Dark curls, tangled and messy. He dropped his hand, oddly annoyed. Hobbs had noticed; Lewis saw his eyes run the length of his body, and he felt his cheeks warm.

'Ah. Yes. I was apologising to you,' Hobbs said, and he had the grace to look sincere.

'There's really no need,' Lewis replied, embarrassed for him.

'Sometimes I...' Hobbs broke off, his face darkening. Lewis sensed he should remain silent. Hobbs was making some sort of decision. He cleared his throat.

'Well, my behaviour is sometimes less than it should be,' he said, abandoning whatever truth he had considered revealing.

Lewis was disappointed. He thought of the meeting, how small he had felt under Hobbs' gaze. He looked up to meet it now and blushed at the way Hobbs was looking at him. Hobbs pushed himself away from the dresser and walked over to the door. Lewis swallowed, felt his irritation dissipate.

'You know, Julie wasn't wrong about the accent,' Hobbs said.

He leaned in and kissed him.

When Lewis woke on Saturday morning, Freddie was gone. A faint smell of cologne lingered in stale air that was otherwise heavy with cigarette smoke. The only tangible evidence of his presence was the discarded tumbler on the sofa, and the soft bruises he had left on Lewis's lips.

Lewis groaned and rubbed vigorously at his left temple, which pulsed unpleasantly under the influence of too much alcohol and too little sleep. His legs were tangled in the bed sheets, and he had to struggle out of them before he could lurch on unsteady feet to the basin. Splashing cool water across his face, he groaned into the depths of the ceramic, and realised he was crying. He dashed an angry hand across his eyes, then washed as quickly as he could.

Within the hour, he was striding along the High Street towards the library. It was closed, being a Saturday, but after three short raps on the back entrance, a short, stocky man opened the door and ushered him in.

'Lewis! It's been a while,' Arthur said, pleasantly surprised. 'We heard you got a promotion. I suppose you've been busy.'

They entered the study room of the library, where an intimate group of two sat around a large round table. Strewn across it was an assortment of playing cards, books and notebooks, while the two people passed between them a bottle of whisky and packets of cigarettes.

'Carson! Christ, we thought we'd rid ourselves of you!' Ken looked a bit drunk as he raised the bottle in Lewis's general direction, spilling a glug on the table in the process.

The young woman next to him broke out in a sweet smile. 'It's nice to see you,' she said.

Lewis nodded at her, unaccountably awkward, sure that his previous night's activities were somehow obvious. He felt himself blush.

'Well? Where have you been hiding? Six weeks it's been, and here I am stuck with a bloody poet and – sorry Ann, but it's true – a silly wee lassie.' Ken ruffled the young woman's hair with what appeared to be affectionate intentions but came across as rather aggressive.

Lewis had once described Ken as 'obnoxiously Scottish', and Ann had nodded gravely. She winced beneath Ken's large hand, quietly trying to smooth out her fair hair as soon as he returned his attention to Lewis. Arthur settled himself at the other end of the table and shot Ken a reproachful frown.

Lewis cleared his throat, nervous. 'Sorry for the radio silence, chaps,' he said, taking a seat next to Ken and deliberately taking the bottle from him. 'But here I am. Ready to share one of those "tortured, pseudo-intellectual" pieces you all love so dearly.' With this he winked at Ann, who chuckled, and he felt some of his bravado return.

'I never said that,' Ken interjected. 'I said they were *torturous* and pseudo-intellectual.'

Lewis felt a twinge of irritation but laughed along with Arthur and Ken. Ann looked vaguely uncomfortable, but then, she was always too sensitive for these group sessions. He often wondered what brought her back, week after week. Ken was invariably drunk and unbearable, he himself was quiet, and even Arthur was subdued and only quietly polite about her work. They were hardly a literary *corp d'elite*, just a ramshackle writers' group with not one published piece between them and a tendency to get drunk before they got constructive.

Ann was an average writer. She produced inoffensive,

36

uninspired samples of a seemingly very long novel on a weekly basis. Arthur had been trying – and failing – to write his *Waste Land*, while Lewis produced short stories one week and ill-judged essays the other. Ken didn't actually contribute any writing of his own, but claimed to bring his expertise as an agent to the table.

Lewis was loath to admit it, for the man was miserable, a drunk and often cruel, but he could be helpful when he wanted to be. The problem was, he repeatedly told Lewis, that he should be writing novels, not short stories or poems. He was a writer who needed 'breadth, space and scope' – *not to mention, son, your shorter stuff is just awful, god-awful.*

'Where *have* you been?' Ann asked, breaking into his thoughts.

'Hmm? Oh – working,' he answered truthfully. 'I'm on the editorial team now.'

'Oh Lewis, that's –'

'Editorial?' Ken interrupted. 'That's a laugh. Freddie Hobbs got you running errands? Making his tea and wiping his a–'

'*Ken.*'

'Sorry, Ann. Lewis knows what I mean, though, eh? A special variety of prick, is our Freddie.'

Lewis felt a flush creep up under his collar and, without thinking, pressed his fingers to his mouth. He was aware of the lengthening silence in the room, Ann's thoughtful gaze and Ken's belligerence. A slight tremble in his leg.

'He isn't so bad,' he offered.

Ken raised a cynical eyebrow but let it pass. 'Well, the

prodigal chose a good day to return,' he said, jostling Arthur's elbow. 'We're celebrating.'

Arthur looked abashed but pleased and ducked his head to both Ann and Ken, who beamed at him.

Lewis tensed. 'Celebrating?' he asked. Ken was watching him, his eyes roving across his face as though searching for something. Lewis threw a questioning glance at Ann, who smiled almost sympathetically.

'Arthur's only gone and secured himself a publisher,' Ken announced, watching him.

Lewis swallowed. Arthur and Ann appeared to be eyeing him warily, and he fixed a bright smile to his face. 'Well, con-gratulations, man!' he managed, slapping Arthur's shoulder. Arthur breathed a small laugh, relieved, and he saw Ann relax. This annoyed him far more than Ken's knowing gaze. Had they expected him to erupt in a temper tantrum? He grinned and grabbed the whisky bottle. 'Tell me all about it,' he said, taking a burning swig.

Three hours later, he emerged into the rain with Ann. He pulled off his coat and attempted to cover both their heads.

'Should we?' Ann shouted up at him, nodding her head in the direction of a steamy café.

He nodded his assent, and they bumped shoulders as they ran across the street. Inside, Ann shook out her damp hair, cheeks pink, and for the first time he thought she might be quite attractive.

They ordered a pot of tea, and he watched her in silence as she stirred two sugar cubes into the milky blend. Their knees rested against one another underneath the small table, and he felt a warmth of companionship with her he rarely felt with anyone else. Ann was sweet and – *God help him for thinking it* – she was terribly impressed by him. They passed the first hour and the first pot of tea talking animatedly about the latest edition of Hobbs' literary magazine – *still only one woman in there, Lewis* – and had ordered another pot by the time the second hour arrived.

'They should have printed your last short, I think.' She looked at him shyly, and he was flattered. He had submitted somewhere in the region of twenty short stories to the magazine over the last year, but each had been declined by the editorial department. *Perhaps after last night, Freddie would* – that tremble again, and he clattered his cup against the teapot, sloshing dark liquid over the side.

'Sorry,' he mumbled, embarrassed, as he mopped up the spillage with a handful of napkins. 'I think I might be hung over.' He made an attempt at a light-hearted chuckle.

'Ah, you *must* be in with the boys. Friday night drinks in the King's Head?' She was smiling fondly, as though she'd been there herself.

'How did you know?' he asked.

'Everyone knows, darling! Well, anyone who wants to be published, anyway. People have been lurking in the King's Head for years, hoping to strike up a conversation with an editor. You didn't notice the hangers-on?'

'No,' he confessed. *He'd been far too busy negotiating his bloody unfathomable relationship with his boss.*

'Look closer next time,' she said, a teasing note in her voice. 'You'll find plenty of adoring fans.'

It was past seven in the evening when Lewis finally walked back along the High Street to his flat. He was carrying a bag of chips as he swung open the gate, whistling as he strode up the path.

'Lewis.'

He stopped in his tracks as Freddie appeared in the doorway.

'I brought some wine,' he said.

They lay in bed, Freddie's leg entangled around Lewis's, Lewis's hand resting in Freddie's fair hair. The bottle of wine sat on the bedside table, half of its contents consumed. The faintest whisper of daylight was beginning to creep through the drapes, but the room was mostly dark, and heavy with cigarette smoke.

The mood in the room was languid, but just beneath the surface, Lewis sensed a certain tension, a quiet hum or vibration, like a chord pulled too tight. And there was his fear. A leaden lump of terror that rose in his throat periodically, only to vanish just as quickly when a hand softly brushed over bare skin, or Freddie's breath kissed a sigh onto his shoulder, where his head rested. These were easy moments, moments that caused his breath to soften and his mind to still – it was the lack of reserve in this touch, though, that when thought about afterwards, seemed like a violation.

The aftermath of their first coupling had brought,

unbidden and startling, the memory of an afternoon on West Cairn Hill with David, the Canadian boy. David's family had immigrated to Canada when he was five years old, but when his father died, he had returned to Edinburgh with his mother and sister and a catalogue of (probably fabricated) bear-related stories that made his company especially valuable to his city-dwelling Scottish classmates. Lewis had forgotten about the boy, but that first bruising kiss from Freddie had awakened in him a distinct memory of David Wells.

Lewis had suggested they spend Sunday afternoon exploring the cairn with the express intention of taking David along the Thieves Road, where his father said the most notorious robbers used to target drovers and their cattle. David had inspired in Lewis a strong desire to impress, and displaying his outdoor hardiness as well as his knowledge of the Pentland Hills had seemed to his thirteen-year-old mind the most suitable way of achieving this desire. But David had been swift in disabusing him of any such notions. He was perhaps three inches taller than Lewis and was therefore quicker and stronger in his stride up the hill. When the smaller boy inevitably began to fall behind, the taller – who was by now projecting a very convincing image of elder superiority – declared he was bored, and lowered himself with an aged sigh onto the damp, flat surface of a green-covered rock. Lewis, peeved and embarrassed, stopped short of this insulting resting place and scuffed his shoes into the peaty ground.

'Do you smoke?' David had asked as he extracted a small, bent cigarette from his inner pocket.

Lewis had shaken his head, mute, shocked, but achingly impressed with the boy's adult glamour. He watched as David lit the match and lowered his dark head away from the wind chill and into the cup of his hands. It took three attempts, but once lit, he puffed on the cigarette with the air of one long initiated.

'Well, take a drag, why don't you?' David said, perhaps because he had tired of the smaller boy's stare.

Lewis took the shrunken white tip and took a deep, too-long inhalation of dirty, thick smoke. David of course laughed when he coughed. Hacking and bent over to his knees, Lewis decided that he hated David. But when a warm, strong hand straightened him and patted his back with a sort of rough affection, he caught himself laughing with him.

Their eyes met, Lewis's streaming from his previous exhortations, and he lost himself for a moment to the glorious rebellion of it all. David hooked his arm around his shoulders and propelled them towards the top of the cairn, where, at the summit, he seemed moderately impressed with Lewis's tales of thieving and night raids.

David was only in their class for three short months following their secret act – that dreadful, lovely cigarette – for his mother remarried quite suddenly and moved them once more, this time to Glasgow. Lewis was for some weeks quite bereft at the loss of his new friend, but soon began to forget the dark-haired Canadian.

He had shared his first kiss with Helen Craig the following summer. An uninspiring, one-off tryst that he didn't enjoy half as much as he led his classmates to believe. He lost his virginity whilst at Edinburgh University, shyly, with a girlfriend who lasted a year but whom he no longer thought about. Her name was Mary; she was a soft-spoken music student, ultimately very boring, and he had no overly fond memories of their time together. She had asked him, several weeks before he ended the relationship, if he still found her attractive.

'Of course I do,' he had responded, not bothering to interrogate whether or not there was any truth in his response.

She had stared at him for a moment, quiet, unconvinced. 'Is there someone else?' she asked.

He had laughed, put down his dinner fork and met her eye across the table. 'Absolutely not. I don't know where this is coming from.'

'No. Perhaps you don't.' She sighed.

It was only now, his hand resting in Freddie's hair, that he realised she was more astute than he had given her credit for.

'He can't write for toffee.'

'In your opinion.'

'The correct opinion.'

'You are *grossly* arrogant, Dickson. I —'

'Enough! The bickering stops now.' Freddie gazed severely across the desk at Dickson and Goldstein, his glasses slung low on his nose and a sheaf of paper curled in his fist. 'This is not some two-bit book group. There will be no squabbling over opinions. We *analyse* here.' A pregnant pause. 'We have

43

voted, Goldstein, and are in agreement that we will not be publishing the Hollinhurst. So. Please do shut up.'

Goldstein flushed, nodded, and adjusted his tie with great fastidiousness. Dickson flashed an apologetic nod towards Freddie and shuffled the papers in front of him.

The editorial meeting had been composed of several such episodes, and a palpable anxiety lay across the room. Lewis caught Julie's eye for a second, shrugged his shoulders to signal exasperation. She turned her chin in the opposite direction. *Oh, for goodness' sake.*

'Finally, we may move on.' Freddie's gaze lingered for a moment on Goldstein's bowed head before he turned to the rest of the editorial team. He did not look directly at Lewis, for which Lewis was glad. His palms felt revoltingly moist underneath the table, and he was sure he was sweating through his shirt.

'I have here a piece from one of our own,' Freddie's sternness vanished quite suddenly and he smiled around the room. 'It is a short essay on poetic translation by Mr Carson here, and I think it merits inclusion in this month's magazine. Thoughts?'

Lewis coughed, his eyes searching the faces of the editorial team for signs of disbelief, or worse, mockery. Julie was certainly startled, casting him a long look he could not quite fathom. She was either impressed, or peeved. He could not tell the difference.

Goldstein, chastened, bobbed his head in assent, but made no further comment. Dickson looked perplexed and was attempting to meet Goldstein's eye, but their earlier spat had clearly disturbed their usual equilibrium, and Goldstein was either unaware of his colleague's appeal or was ignoring it. Lewis thought that the latter was most likely the case.

'Give me strength,' Freddie sighed. 'For two hours you have squabbled like infants, but now you have nothing to say?'

Lewis nervously cracked his knuckle, and the group as a whole turned to look at him. He flushed.

'It needs some work. I understand if people are hesitant.' He shrugged, wishing to look modest.

Freddie frowned, annoyed. 'No one said anything of the sort,' he said. 'Dickson. You've read the essay. What did you think?'

'Oh, promising, sir. A bit *academic*, perhaps. But with a good edit, a fine essay, yes.'

'We are nothing if not academic,' Goldstein muttered.

'Please,' Freddie said, a note of warning in his voice. Goldstein's chin was practically resting on his bellybutton. A short silence ensued.

'Good. We are in agreement, then. Carson's essay will lead the Reviews section next month.'

This signalled the end of the editorial meeting. Goldstein was the first to leave his chair, bolting for the door like a frightened rabbit. Dickson looked regretfully about the room before following him, an apology already half-formed on his lips. Subdued murmurs punctuated the sound of chairs scraping against the floor as the remaining employees shuffled from the room. Julie smiled at Lewis as she exited, and he was glad to be friends again. Lewis remained in his seat, as did Freddie, until they were alone in the room.

They sat for several minutes, contemplating one another across the table.

'Thank you,' Lewis said.

'I didn't do it because of us, if that's what you think.'

Lewis gazed steadily at him.

'Well, not strictly because of that,' Freddie conceded.

'Thank you,' Lewis repeated.

Freddie smiled. 'Should I close the door?' he asked.

Lewis sighed. 'Not here, surely.'

Freddie's smile faded.

'I only mean that we haven't discussed anything,' Lewis said. 'I'm not sure... I'm not sure what we're doing, exactly.'

Freddie nodded, pursed his lips. He stood and closed the door anyway.

'I'm the first?' he asked, appearing neither proud nor shocked, which Lewis appreciated.

'Yes.' Lewis gathered a modicum of courage. 'And I for you?'

'No. I'm sorry, but no.'

'Oh. No need to apologise.' Lewis looked down at his fingertips and scratched ineffectually at a catch of skin on his thumb.

'Cambridge...' Freddie trailed off, a troubled look on his face.

Oh, Lewis thought. The head of department? Someone else, perhaps. Someone important enough that Freddie felt compelled to leave. This ate at him for a moment as he considered his own feelings. It bothered him that Freddie might have felt this about someone other than himself. He stopped the thought in its tracks. What *did* Freddie feel? Lewis only knew that he himself felt at once elated, sick, troubled and overwhelmed whilst aching for his touch again. He had assumed Freddie felt the same, was as taken aback by their feelings as he was. But perhaps not. Perhaps he was just one of…

Lewis was aware that Freddie had moved to the back of his chair, and he sighed with pleasure as Freddie's hand gathered in the hair at the nape of his neck. Freddie leaned over him and rested soft lips against his cheek.

'You are important,' he murmured, as though reading his thoughts.

Lewis closed his eyes as Freddie's lips traced lightly down his neck. His arousal was clear, and he heard Freddie's breath quicken as he reached down to release his belt buckle. He had almost tugged it open when there was a sharp knock at the door.

They leapt apart, burnt, startled, guilty.

Julie allowed several seconds to pass before she entered the room. *She knows*, Lewis thought. *She knows*.

'Sorry to interrupt,' she said, clearly anything but. She appraised them both, pink cheeks on each and Freddie standing breathless two feet behind Lewis's chair.

'You haven't interrupted, Julie. Not to worry. How can I help you?' Freddie's vocal composure was sound. Polite and distant. But she wasn't fooled. Lewis knew, from the lingering gaze she directed at him to the faint smile that parted her lips as she looked back and forth between the two of them. She fucking *knew*.

'I just needed you to sign off on this layout before we begin the final typesetting. A quick signature would be lovely, Mr Hobbs.'

'Of course. Certainly.' Lewis realised Freddie did not want to step away from behind the chair. His own erection was obscured by the desk in front of him, but Freddie had no such luxury. Julie waved the paperwork expectantly, her eyes dancing. *The bitch. The goddamn bitch.* A short pause, then Freddie laughed, embarrassed and self-effacing.

'Forgive me. It's been a testing morning. Let me sign those for you.' He sidestepped the chair and, mercifully, Lewis could see no physical sign of their almost-encounter as he accepted the papers from Julie. He bent over the desk and began signing. Over their boss's back, Julie gave Lewis a radiant and vindictive smile.

Shit.

Fuck.

She knows.

✳

The weeks passed. They fucked. They smoked cigarettes in Lewis's room. They ate cold picnics on the bed. Freddie brought expensive cuts of cheese and continental meats, and Lewis bought cheap wine. On the nights Freddie was absent, Lewis shut himself in the flat and smoked cigarettes, at a loss on what to do with himself.

He fretted over Julie, an anxiety Freddie dismissed with increasing irritation. It became clear he had no patience for these discussions, and it was the only time they came close to arguing with one another.

Lewis discovered that for the most part, he would talk and Freddie would listen, quiet, interested, his hands playing with strands of Lewis's hair. They spoke about his mother, whom he loved, and about his father, of whom Lewis spoke with less warmth. Freddie seemed particularly interested in the girlfriend, Mary, expressing a strange sort of sympathy for her that made Lewis defensive.

But for the most part, they talked about books and writers. Where Freddie was reluctant to reveal details of his own life (that university lover held back from him in an act of sheer malice, Lewis felt), he was full of gossip from the literary hoi polloi. There was an agent at Cabot Circus who was known to make promises in return for certain financial and sexual favours – promises he never fulfilled in kind. There were rumours that Graham Church, a celebrated young novelist on the rise, had a problem with alcohol and that he would soon be dropped by his publisher.

Freddie was full of opinions, too, on the merits or failings of the city's most respected writers. Kitty Jacob was the most talented novelist writing in England, he claimed, but would never be as successful as she ought to be because she insisted on having 'countless idiot children'. Dorothy Fleming was equally talented, but too insubstantial – she was only a quiet spinster. Lewis had never met her and asked what age she was. *Thirty-eight*, Freddie snorted, and Lewis felt chilled.

But Freddie's greatest monologues were reserved for the novelist Balmer, about whom he spoke with passionate disdain. *Like a squalling infant at his mother's breast – hungry, angry, insensitive to anything but his own loud voice in an otherwise quiet room.* That Balmer was read widely and respected by critics and his peers seemed to anger him, and Lewis had wondered more than once – cursing his idiocy and childish jealousy – whether their relationship were somehow more intimate than that of author and reader. But he never dared to ask and would instead seek to prop up Freddie's anger, preferring that he disdain the man than confess a more personal reason for his aggravation.

Only once had he asked Freddie to read one of his own samples, the opening chapter of a novel he had begun writing a year ago but had not touched for many weeks. It had been an uncomfortable experience. Freddie was enthusiastic, perhaps even warm in his praise, but it became clear that Lewis had craved more. After an increasingly fraught conversation about the intricacies of one scene, Freddie had discarded the manuscript on the floor and made it clear that he had no interest in massaging Lewis's ego. Their fucking had been rough, almost violent that night. Knowing it to be a futile exercise in vanity, Lewis had not asked him to read anything again; Freddie would not gush if he did not feel justified in doing so, and besides, Lewis hadn't written anything new since they had started.

Many evenings they were joined by Mrs Bell. They would play cards, her inappropriate stories of Lawrence Hobbs punctuated by simpering requests for more sherry. Lewis tolerated her – indeed, found her fascinating at times – while Freddie delighted in her presence. This puzzled Lewis, for half of the stories were clearly fiction, and those which were not were embarrassing, painting a portrait of a hard-drinking, hard-loving man who took pleasure in discrediting his family's solid reputation. It struck him that this appealed to Freddie, and he realised without feeling too petulant that perhaps he was serving as Freddie's own quiet rebellion against the Hobbs family name.

Without noticing, a month had passed.

They were careful in the office, rarely speaking to one another, polite and cool when they were forced to. But always there was Julie. A walking smirk, all knowing looks and swinging hips, winking at him throughout every editorial meeting and looking intently at Freddie when she wasn't doing that.

Finally, Freddie noticed. Lewis felt vindicated, even gloated that he'd been more perceptive. Fool. It was only the beginning of the end. What was there to gloat over in that?

II

June twelfth was Ken's birthday. He had asked Lewis and Ann to L'Etoile on Charlotte Street, and then they were to meet eight or ten others at his house for a small party. Lewis left the flat in a hurry sometime after six in the evening, Ken's gift – a book – wrapped in blue tissue and tucked into his pocket. He left Freddie in his bed.

'Who's your date?' he had asked.

'Ann. But she's not my date.'

'Poor Ann.'

Lewis bent and brushed a kiss on Freddie's lips, more to shut him up than to be affectionate, and hastened out the door.

He was not in a good mood. He had planned to shave and put on a fresh suit, but Freddie had arrived uninvited shortly after work, and as Lewis walked along the street now he realised he smelled of cigarette smoke and sweat. He had not had time to shave, either, and his chin and jaw were dark with stubble. He wished Freddie hadn't come over, a fact which surprised him.

Ann met him at the bus stop, pretty in a blue dress. She was wearing lipstick and had pinned her hair back, and he told her she looked lovely. Blushing, she took his arm and did not let go for the duration of the bus ride to Soho.

Ken was already at the table when they arrived, cheerful and smiling. He chucked Lewis under the chin and told him he couldn't pull off a beard before kissing Ann's cheek and ushering her into a seat.

'Happy birthday, darling,' Ann said, passing him a slim box, which he opened immediately.

'A handsome scarf for a handsome man, eh? Thank you, Annie, it's perfect.'

The silk Paisley scarf looked expensive, and Lewis was a little shamefaced as he handed over the book wrapped in tissue. It was a pocket poetry collection – Scottish poets – and he had written a brief note on the inner leaf wishing Ken a happy thirtieth.

'That's really something,' Ken said, and he seemed genuine.

They ordered a bottle of red wine and spoke in low voices about the rising stage actor who was dining at a table near the door. Ann was happy, and Lewis began to forget that he was in a bad mood. It felt nice to be away from Freddie, he realised. The restaurant was relatively small and it was busy, but it felt bigger and fresher than his flat, where he had spent too many evenings of late, so he decided to enjoy the company and made jokes with Ann about Ken's imminent retirement, which Ken took in good spirits.

'How's the job?' Ken asked.

'Busy. More admin than editorial, to tell you the truth,' Lewis said, as casually as he could.

'I had a drink with that fellow Goldstein over the weekend.'

'Oh?'

'Don't look so concerned. He only had good things to say about you,' Ken said.

Lewis wondered why Ken would be drinking with Goldstein but didn't fancy talking about his Hobbs colleagues lest things stray in Freddie's direction. Instead, he asked Ann about work. She had a sales job in one of the big department stores, but he could never remember which one.

She shrugged. 'I sell gloves.'

They ordered another bottle of wine and gossiped about Arthur's upcoming poetry publication. Ann scolded them both for being insincere but couldn't help but laugh when Ken described the poem as 'a warm shit in a cold room'.

'What does that even *mean*?' she asked.

Lewis paid the bill, wincing internally at the price, but he couldn't allow Ann or the birthday boy to pay. By the time they reached Ken's townhouse, Lewis was pleasantly tipsy. He knew some of the other guests, mostly writers and other publishing colleagues. Ann remained by his side almost constantly, and he introduced her as his good friend, unsure whether that was the right phrase for it. People seemed to assume they were a couple, and as he watched the reactions of men who had not met her before, he realised he didn't mind the assumption. Ann did indeed look lovely, and Lewis noted the way they watched her, how attentive they seemed. He began to enjoy himself and even put his arm around her waist. She leaned into him, happy.

His good mood vanished when Ken ushered two new guests into the reception room, a man and a woman. She had not yet seen him, but the woman was Julie Sutherland. She kissed Ken on the lips and they laughed as she wiped a smear of red lipstick from his mouth. Her companion gently pulled her back, perhaps feeling possessive.

'Do you know them?' Ann asked, catching his gaze.

He looked down at her, uneasy.

'She works at Hobbs,' he said. 'Not a nice a woman.'

Ann frowned and looked over at Julie, who had finally spotted Lewis. She broke into a wide smile and made her way across the room, leaving her date stuck in conversation with Ken and staring after her.

'Darling! Fancy seeing you here.'

She treated him to the same performance he had already witnessed on Ken, leaning in to deliberately kiss his mouth, then glancing at Ann and laughing as she rubbed the red mark from his lips.

'Ann Barbour, this is Julie Sutherland. Julie, this is my good friend Ann.'

Ann stuck her hand out, perhaps hoping to avoid a kiss, but Julie merely pulled the smaller woman towards her by the wrist and bumped a hard kiss on her cheek. Ann rubbed self-consciously at the spot as she pulled back. Julie looked them up and down, noting his arm around Ann's waist.

'You must be Lewis's secret friend,' she said, winking.

'Secret?' Ann asked.

Not wishing to play, Lewis cleared his throat and passed Julie a glass of champagne from the drinks table behind them.

'So how do you know Ken?' he asked, hoping to distract

her. She took a sip of her drink and winked at him.

'He so hates to talk about himself, doesn't he, Ann?'

'Um, I—'

'That's fine,' Julie interrupted. 'We're all entitled to our private lives. What were you asking, Lewis? How do I know Ken? Oh, I don't, not really. He's Walter's agent,' she said, nodding over at her date, who was still talking to Ken. The man seemed to sense her gaze and looked over, then gestured for her to return to him. She sighed. 'I suppose I should go tell him how wonderful he is.'

She turned back and smiled at Ann. 'You don't have to worry about that with Lewis, of course.'

'I don't?'

'Lewis can actually write, unlike poor Walter. Well, so Frederick tells us. Speaking of, I heard through the grape-vine that we might be printing one of your short stories in next month's issue. Frederick is very excited about you.'

'Lewis, you didn't tell me!' Ann jostled his arm and he laughed awkwardly.

'I'm afraid it's news to me too,' he said, staring at Julie and trying to determine if she was lying.

'Oh, I'm sure Frederick just wants to give you the good news himself.'

'Perhaps.'

Lewis sipped at his champagne, willing her to leave. She smiled at him, seemingly aware of his discomfort.

'Well. Back to dear Walter I go. Enjoy your night, love-birds. What a lovely couple you make.'

She winked and left them without another word. Lewis

removed his arm from Ann's waist, who looked up at him with a frown.

'She seems nice,' she said, her tone uncertain.

'No, she's really not.'

Lewis exhaled slowly, a plume of smoke spiralling into the air above his head. He was lying on his bed in the dark, drapes open and pale moonlight spilling across his face. The cigarette was burning his throat, but he continued to take long, dry draws of it. A plate of cold ham and eggs lay unappetising on the dresser alongside an uncorked bottle of wine. Not much of the wine was left, though the plate remained untouched.

His eyes moved from the ceiling to the door as, for the third time that evening, Mrs Bell's heels stuttered to a stop at his door. She rattled the doorknob.

'Lewis,' she called.

'I'm quite alright, Mrs Bell,' he said, somewhat tartly, and did not move from his bed. She was silent for a moment, though she shifted from one foot to the other as though contemplating further conversation. Finally, she gave up and departed down the stairs.

Lewis returned to his quiet observation of the smoke plume. He felt somewhat undone, his sense of self dissipating at the seams, pressed down by his thoughts.

Freddie was at dinner with Julie.

He sat up and stubbed out the cigarette on the edge of the dresser, leaving an angry scorch mark. He immediately felt bad, his eyes darting over to the door in case Mrs Bell's heels were silhouetted in the gap there. *Self-indulgent*, he chided himself.

He made a decision.

He rose from the bed and switched on the small table lamp. In the dimness drawn by the glow, he surveyed the mess he had left on the desk and shuffled the stacks of paperwork into orderly piles. At the top was a short manuscript bearing Ann's neat handwriting. He dropped into the desk chair and angled the lamp directly over the text. Perhaps this week he would read it properly; she would appreciate his feedback in particular, he knew. He ignored her short summary and turned to the first page of the writing proper, drawing his wine glass over and settling into the task.

On the last day of the twentieth century, the stars in the sky collectively fell, black and dead, and the world became their tomb.

He drew himself up, surprised.

The young woman watched them drop and knew that she was now the only soul left in the universe.

Lewis flicked through the pages, nonplussed. She had rewritten the entire thing, he realised. It was better. Perhaps even quite good. Her prior drafts had been terse, unfeeling nonsenses about a lonely spinster. This was more interesting by far. He sat immersed in the pages for some time, making notes in the margins that were kinder than he would permit anyone else. Her heroine was prone to bouts of tedious gloom, but otherwise he found something starkly beautiful about the text. He was scribbling an enquiry when his doorknob rattled once more, and he turned, irritated.

'Mrs Bell, I really am quite alright!' He was aware of how unpleasant his tone was and did not regret it.

'I'm sure you are, dear,' she said, her voice muffled by the door. 'I've only come to tell you that you have a visitor,' she added, affecting a tone of affront now, no doubt for the benefit of said visitor.

Lewis sprang to the door, certain it was Freddie. It must be Freddie. Julie wouldn't –

He stopped as Mrs Bell wobbled sideways and Ken appeared, grinning, at her shoulder.

'Kenneth,' he said, a bit dully. Ken strode past Mrs Bell. She giggled, and Lewis thought Ken might have brushed his hand against her backside.

'Your brother has been telling me about your writers' group, Lewis,' Mrs Bell said, manoeuvring towards the doorway as if she was going to join them.

'Brother?' Lewis parroted, face aghast.

Ken laughed, a loud and obnoxious intrusion in the small, quiet room.

'Oh, no, Mrs Bell!' he assured her, not at all offended by Lewis's apparent horror. 'I might hail from the North, but we're not related. I'm a Glasgow man,' he added, lean-ing towards her with a wink. 'Real spit and sawdust town. We're not so genteel as these Edinburgh boys.' Lewis looked sharply at him, wondering if the emphasis on that last word – *boys* – had been deliberate. But Ken grinned at him, innocent.

'What are you doing here?' Lewis asked, and Mrs Bell tutted. Recalling his manners, he added, 'Not that I'm not glad to see you. I was spending a rather miserable night at my desk with Ann's book.'

'Aye, that does sound miserable,' Ken said, though he looked over at the desk with some interest. 'I'm taking you for a drink,' he said, propelling them all out of the door and into the hallway. Mrs Bell's shoe caught on the edge of the carpet and she stumbled, jostled too quickly by Ken's large frame. Lewis reached out and steadied her, and he saw her throw a stern look at Ken.

'Well, do be quiet when you come home, Lewis,' she said. Ken, realising he had lost some of her good will, bowed deeply to her. It was a patronising move, and Mrs Bell's jaw clenched.

'I'll have him home nice and early, Mrs Bell,' he promised, his smile mocking. She merely nodded and tottered up the main stairwell, evidently climbing up to the attic level to bother someone else.

'Christ,' Ken muttered, and nudged Lewis's arm.

'She's an excellent landlady,' Lewis responded, inexplicably annoyed.

Ken snorted and made for the stairs, indicating that Lewis should follow with a wave of his hand.

They ended up in the King's Head, suggested by Lewis to satisfy some perverse desire to be near the office, though he knew Freddie would of course be elsewhere. Would they be talking about him? The thought made him uncomfortable, which in turn tended to make him fidget. He closed his left hand around his right wrist, stilling its unconscious tremor under the table.

As a child, these nervous tics had been more pronounced. When called upon to approach the blackboard in primary school, both hands would shake so much that the teacher would often have to write his answers for him. Lewis would walk back to his desk with his hands jammed into his trouser pockets, his cheeks red, exacerbating the snide laughter of his classmates. His father was incensed by these near-constant trembles, in particular the way in which he bobbed his ankle up and down under the dinner table, nervous under his father's stare. He checked his foot now, self-conscious, and was pleased that it remained still. God forbid Freddie ever witness such anxiety.

Ken sank into the chair opposite, two pints in hand, distracting Lewis from further agitation. He was putting on weight, Lewis thought, as he mopped at the sheen of sweat on his face. They drank in silence for a moment as Ken took in the bar clientele.

'This is where your lot come?' he asked, jerking his head at a group of men at the bar who might have been Hobbs employees. Lewis didn't recognise any of them, but nodded nonetheless.

'Aye, they've got that look about them.' For the second time that night, Lewis wondered if Ken was trying to imply something. But he was drinking his pint, innocent, and Lewis decided he was being paranoid.

'I wanted to speak to you in private,' Ken said, putting his pint down and leaning towards him with an earnest look. Lewis stared back at him.

'Oh?' he managed.

'What do you make of Arthur?' Ken asked.

Oh, Lewis thought. He sat back, a defensive move, and wondered if Ken wished merely to rub his face in Arthur's success.

'I think he's an able writer. I'm glad for him,' he said, the words sounding feeble even to himself.

Ken snorted. 'He's not half the writer you could be,' he said, surprising Lewis.

He eyed Ken across the table, suspicious, and took a drink of his pint. He didn't answer.

'I've come across a bit of an opportunity. Chap at Crothers owes me a favour. I want to send him one of your manuscripts, act as your agent.'

Lewis felt his pulse quicken. He took another drink, assessing Ken over the rim of the glass before he answered.

'And why would you want to do that?' he asked.

Ken shrugged, affecting nonchalance, but his bearing betrayed his eagerness as he leaned back across the table. 'You left one of your samples at the library the other day,' he replied, his eyes bright. 'It's… Christ, Lewis, it's the one. It's a bestseller, I'm sure of it. An award winner, maybe.' He looked almost feverish as he gulped down the lukewarm bitter.

Lewis frowned, trying to recall what he'd taken to the library. He hadn't written anything for weeks. After all, until the Thursday evening when they'd argued so furiously about Julie, Freddie had been something of a permanent fixture in his room. He had been distracted. *He's with her now*, the traitorous thought ran through his mind. *You behaved like a jealous infant and now he's with her*. He set it aside, angry, and realised suddenly what Ken was talking about. He had conducted a meeting on the Friday morning, still simmering from his and Freddie's argument.

Oh.

Fran Watson.

He closed his eyes for a moment, not quite ashamed but at least embarrassed at the memory. She had been a walk-in, dowdy and anxious and underwhelming, and he had taken his frustration with Freddie out on her, been cool, unfriendly. Perhaps even patronising. He had taken the manuscript home and promised to read it, though he had no authority to do so – a petty act of defiance against his job description. Watson had an appointment to exchange feedback in a fortnight or so, if he recalled correctly. He hadn't read it, of course, his mind too wrapped up in his own petty jealousies. It must have been amongst the papers he removed from his bag the next morning at their writers' meeting. Ken wasn't excited by one of his own samples – he was excited by Fran Watson's book. Lewis thought for an alarming moment that he might cry.

'Which manuscript?' he asked finally, a dull hope taking hold that perhaps he was mistaken.

'*Infinite Eden,*' Ken said.

Ah.

'It's really something, Lewis. Let me take it to Crothers. They've just done well with Cummings' new book – good publishers. I can agent you. We'll both benefit here.' His words were rushed, pleading almost, betraying his own self-interest.

Lewis pinched the bridge of his nose and decided that Ken either hadn't spotted Watson's name on the front page of the manuscript sample or thought it was some sort of pseudonym.

'Ken, it's not —'

'Think about it!' Ken interjected, plainly reading the negative response. Lewis sighed, made to open his mouth and speak, but Ken put his hand in the air to stop him. 'Just think about it, alright? This is the one, Carson. This is your debut.'

Lewis shut his mouth. He was too dulled to argue. Dulled by Freddie, dulled by Fran Watson. He finished his pint in silence, a dismal throbbing behind his eyes, his mind elsewhere.

Ken insisted on walking him back to the flat and postulated expansively on their imminent success. Lewis tried to shush him as they approached the front door, but Ken was unflappable, determined perhaps to win him over by sheer force of enthusiasm.

'And there's Arthur,' he snorted, 'thinking he's won a watch with a puny poem in Low's!'

Lewis bit off his reply when Freddie appeared in front of them on the shaded pathway. He was upset, quite visibly. His hair was a wavy tangle and he was holding his glasses in a clenched fist. No tie, no jacket, just a crumpled white shirt with its sleeves rolled above the elbow and the top two buttons undone.

Ken peered at him through the gloom and stopped short. 'Hobbs?' he asked, incredulous.

Freddie seemed to shudder, and he looked at them both with a wild air of suspicion that made Lewis blanch. *He couldn't think….?*

'It is too,' Ken said. 'Been upstairs with Mrs Bell, have you?' he continued, finding himself hilarious.

'We need to talk,' Freddie said, ignoring Ken and staring impenetrably at Lewis.

Ken's laugh faded and he looked at them, his brow furrowed. 'Everything alright?' he asked, finally sensing the tension. Freddie spared him an irritated glare.

'Just a work thing,' Lewis said, the lie profoundly obvious to them all.

Ken sniffed and began to back off down the path. 'Well, I'll leave you to it,' he said, edging out of the gate. 'Just think about what I said, Carson.'

'Will do, Ken. Goodnight.'

The two men stared at one another for several beats. Ken's footsteps retreated off into the distance, and the faint sound of him whistling soon fell to silence.

'What's happened?' Lewis asked.

Freddie laughed, but it was tinged with hysteria, not mirth. 'Upstairs. *Please*,' he said, his voice hoarse.

They crept up the stairwell as silently as they could, and Mrs Bell mercifully remained absent. Lewis ushered Freddie into the room and locked the door. Turning to face him, he was caught off-guard by Freddie's weight against him, and they fell back against the door with a thud.

'What are –'

He stopped, Freddie's mouth suddenly on his, bruising and desperate. He felt Freddie pull at his hair and he gasped for breath. Something was wrong. It was too needy, too intense. He tried to push Freddie away gently but he merely pulled him closer, Lewis's lower lip caught in a stinging bite.

'Ah! Fuck!' Lewis moved once more to push him away, and Freddie pinned his arm against the doorframe.

Despite himself, Lewis felt his body respond. He wrapped his free arm around Freddie's waist and they half-stumbled, half-dragged one another towards the bed. Just as they reached its edge, Lewis remembered himself. Julie's face appeared in his mind, a stabbing reminder, and he roughly pushed Freddie away. He fell onto the bed in a sitting position, and Lewis took two strides back, wiping at his bloodied lip.

'Stop,' Lewis said, his voice deadly.

Freddie burst into tears. Lewis stood, confounded, unsure of himself. He took in a dark graze on Freddie's forearm, the tousled hair, and felt cold dread steal over him.

'What happened tonight?' he asked again.

Freddie let out a last rasping sob before calming himself. He helped himself to a sip of the wine still on Lewis's desk and made a futile attempt to smooth his hair.

'You were right,' he said, throwing him an almost hateful glance. 'She does know. And she saw right through my flir-tation with her.'

Lewis closed his eyes and rocked back on his heels. There was no savouring the vindication, he thought. He didn't want to be right.

'I took her to dinner. I was sure that if I deflected her, made her think I was attracted to her, that she would assume she was wrong about us.'

'I told you she's not an idiot,' Lewis said. Freddie snorted disdainfully. Lewis ignored that. 'So how did you leave it?' Given Freddie's state of dress, he wasn't sure he wanted to know the answer.

Freddie was crying again.

'Freddie,' he said, his voice low.

Freddie got up from the bed and strode over to him. His breath smelled of wine and tobacco. He grazed Lewis's jaw with his thumb and kissed him.

'Please,' Freddie whispered against him. 'Please let's forget her for now.'

Lewis cursed himself as he felt himself pull Freddie closer. It was unfair, to make him feel so desperately needed. It was unfair. They fell back onto the bed, and he forgot about Julie.

Edinburgh, 1998

Two days after he met Barbara in the café, Lewis received a visitor.

Ken looked almost gaunt, the heft of his youth long since melted off his bones. His face was permanently tinged pink, a series of burst blood vessels forming a delicate map across his nose and jowls. Lewis made them coffees in the kitchen, and they sat at the table there, rather than have Ken struggle up the stairs to the study.

He had not had to travel far; like Lewis, he had returned to Scotland shortly after his sixtieth, bought a large house in Marchmont. He lived alone, a lifelong bachelor. Sarah pitied his loneliness, and Lewis knew that she sometimes called on him. It was Sarah, he assumed, who had told him about his spell in the café, Sarah who no doubt asked him to call in for a visit.

Ken had brought a printout of Ann's interview with him and spread it flat now on the table in front of Lewis.

'I knew you'd want to read it,' he said by way of explanation.

Lewis nodded his thanks, though in truth he wasn't sure if he did. 'Have you seen her?'

'Every Sunday afternoon. I take her the papers and make her lunch. She's doing well.'

Lewis wasn't much interested in Ann. When he tried to summon a memory of their last meeting, he found he couldn't – it was certainly after Sarah's wedding, but he couldn't be more specific. She had been vibrant at the wedding: stylish in a bright dress, her grey hair long and loose, the uniform of someone trying to self-identify as an ageing bohemian. They had seen one another perhaps a handful of times in the years afterwards, certainly on Sarah's thirtieth birthday and at the funeral of a mutual friend. He was sure the very last time had been more humdrum, but he could not remember the details. He only recalled that she had looked thin, and her hair had been cut short in a style he associated with much older women. It might even have been permed. It had shocked him at the time, the displacement of his image of her as a middle-aged woman, replaced now with one of elderly frailty. Looking at Ken now, though, Lewis supposed they had all changed.

Turning his attention to the article, he skimmed through the first few questions. It was focused on gender inequality in publishing, a subject with which Ann had always been passionately engaged. Her answers certainly seemed lucid, right enough, just as Barbara had said. As he continued reading, his mouth pursed in distaste. The interviewer had changed approach, the questions becoming more personal. His own name leapt out at him, distracting him from thoughts of the journalist.

You met your husband at a writers' group, and your first novel was published within a year of his debut [Barbour was married to celebrated novelist Lewis Carson for 34 years. They separated in 1989]. Your biographer has hinted at his heavy influence on your work during this time.

He certainly inspired me. His success was something I craved for myself, and I'm not ashamed to admit that.

You've always been fairly candid about that period in both your careers, and yet Mr Carson has distanced himself from it. Why do you think that is?

Victory Lap *was such a stunning debut. It catapulted Lewis into the public consciousness and he was thankful for that. But eventually, it became a sort of paper prison to him. That's what he called it, I think – his paper cell. It strangled him, overshadowed every success. Everything always came back to* Victory Lap. *That book was his cell. He never really left it, I think.*

Lewis swallowed and slid the printout away from him.

These were not words a journalist had put in her mouth – they were his words. Bitter words, spat at her in anger and frustration over years of crippling self-doubt. His paper cell indeed. *Damn that book to hell.*

Ken was watching him from across the kitchen table. As though he might erase its words, he folded and quartered the article and stowed it away in his jacket pocket.

'She doesn't know, does she?' he asked, carefully looking at his coffee cup rather than at Lewis.

Lewis blinked at him, surprised. 'Know what?' he responded.

'Lewis,' Ken met his eye, his tone flat. 'She doesn't know about *Infinite Eden*.'

Lewis stilled, his breath slow and weak in the silence. They had never spoke of it, not once in all the years. He had even begun to wonder if perhaps Ken hadn't known, had never seen the name on the front of the manuscript.

'No,' he said, finally. 'I could never tell her. She resented my secrets, and I resented her for trying to pry them from me. It's why I left, in the end.'

Ken nodded, satisfied. Lewis realised that he had been concerned. Ann's newfound candour threatened them both, he supposed.

'What possessed you to arrange the *Herald* interview?' Ken asked then, a question he hadn't expected. Sarah had most certainly called on him.

Lewis shrugged, embarrassed. 'Vanity,' he said, simply.

'Quite. You always were overly concerned with what people thought of you.'

Lewis was annoyed, primarily because he knew it to be true. It was disquieting, the perceptiveness with which Ken spoke these days. He was too sombre, too astute, too self-possessing. The raucous man he had once been was being ground down by a gnawing cancer that ate the flesh from his bones and the warmth of humour from his personality. Ken was dying, and it had made a serious man of him.

'Don't bring it all tumbling down now,' he said, a plea rather than an instruction.

'No,' Lewis agreed.

'We'll have to remain in your paper cell for a bit longer yet,' Ken concluded, only the slightest note of irony in his voice.

London, 1953

'Lewis!' Mrs Bell's voice was shrill as she rattled against his door. 'Mr Carson, wake up, now!'

'Shit, shit, shit,' Lewis whispered, tumbling out from under the sheets and dragging on his trousers. He moved to shake Freddie awake and was half relieved, half disappointed to see that the other side of the bed was empty. He dragged a hand through his hair and jogged across the living room floor.

He threw the door wide, forgetting that he hadn't yet put on a shirt. Mrs Bell eyed him in shock, while the two policemen behind her exchanged glances. Mrs Bell's gaze travelled from his bare torso to the tangled bedsheets, and her mouth compressed into a hard, flat line.

'These two gentlemen wish to speak to you.'

He gaped at her, trying to piece together the why of it.

'Of course,' he said, standing aside to let them enter.

Mrs Bell peered at them for a moment and then turned on her heel, obviously disappointed that she wouldn't be privy to their conversation.

'Thank you, Mrs Bell!' Lewis called, a feeble attempt to curry some favour.

She didn't turn around. He closed the door and turned to face the two policemen, awkwardly thrusting his hands into his pockets and wishing dearly he knew where his shirt was.

'Um.' He swallowed. 'I'd offer you some tea…'

'No need, Mr Carson. We won't take up too much of your time.' The sergeant had removed his hat and was surveying the messy room with a grave expression.

Lewis noted the plate of ham and eggs and decided he wouldn't care to accept tea from such a slattern either.

'Do take a seat,' he said, gesturing towards the unmade bed.

The sergeant looked like he might laugh but merely waved his hand. 'Thank you, but we shan't be long. We have some questions regarding a colleague of yours. Well, colleagues,' he amended. The shorter of the two had retrieved a notebook and pen from his pocket and stood poised and silent.

Lewis rubbed at his eyes. 'Of course. Which colleagues?'

'A Mr Frederick Hobbs and a Ms Julie Sutherland.'

Oh.

'What about them?'

He felt a sudden chill, and yet a sweat had sprung under his arms.

'Julie Sutherland was found dead by her flatmate early this morning, sir.'

He leaned hard against the door, muttered an expletive under his breath. *Oh, Freddie, what have you done?*

He thought about the graze on Freddie's forearm. Lying in the dark last night, he'd touched it lightly and asked if it hurt. Freddie hadn't answered. He hadn't answered any of Lewis's questions about the dinner except to state that she knew – *she knew* – in a dull, flat tone.

He looked up at the two policemen and shrugged helplessly. He opened his mouth more than once to ask a question before shutting it again.

'What happened to her?' he finally managed.

'The circumstances are suspicious, I'm afraid, Mr Carson,' – a brief pause – 'Ms Sutherland's flatmate informed us that she dined with Frederick Hobbs last night. Do you know if that's the case?'

The policeman was watching him carefully. Lewis swallowed. If they'd already spoken to Freddie and he'd lied, what would he be doing by contradicting him? Why were they even *here*, questioning him? He smoothed his hair and met the man's eye.

'Yes,' he said. 'I believe they did have dinner together.'

The silent officer scribbled a note on his pad, nodding to himself. Was that the right answer, then, Lewis wondered?

'Mr Hobbs has indicated to us that he left Ms Sutherland alive and well at Guido's restaurant at around 9pm, and that he met you here to discuss a work matter at roughly 9.30pm. Can you confirm that, Mr Carson?'

Lewis stilled. *You bastard*, he thought. *You utter bastard.* Consciously smoothing his expression, he nodded.

'That sounds about right,' he said.

'And he remained here to discuss that work matter until around 3am this morning?' A sceptical tone, unmistakable and tinged with sarcasm, was evident in the policeman's voice now.

Lewis glanced at the paperwork on his desk and their eyes followed.

'It's not so unusual,' he answered, mustering a grim sort of smile. The note-taker smirked, onside.

'Quite,' the senior officer said. 'And that explains why you're not in work this morning, Mr Carson.'

Lewis blinked, startled. 'What time is it?' he asked.

'Just gone twenty minutes past ten, sir,' the note-taker said, pulling his sleeve back down over his watch.

'Fuck! Sorry.'

The two exchanged glances. Lewis ignored them and began throwing his sheets to the side, lifting three pillows before he found his shirt.

'I'm sorry, I have to go,' he said, stuffing an arm into the wrong sleeve, tutting, removing it and trying again.

'Of course,' the senior officer said, glancing at his colleague before moving towards the door. 'You've confirmed what Mr Hobbs told us this morning. Thank you very much for your time.'

Lewis nodded absently, his eyes searching the room for some socks. As they opened the door to leave, he stopped his search and spoke without thinking.

'Julie – how did she die?'

The senior paused in the doorway, turned to him with a grave expression.

'She was strangled, Mr Carson.'

Edinburgh, 1998

Lewis wasn't sure when the absurd idea had taken such hold of him, but now that it was fixed in his mind, he was unable to dissuade himself from it.

A biography, a complete retrospective of his life and work, to be published in his seventieth year.

It had been three weeks since he first met Barbara in the café. He couldn't claim to admire her, nor was he very familiar with her work at the *Herald*. In truth, he disliked her very much and suspected that she didn't particularly like him. Perversely, it was this that made her, to his mind, an ideal candidate to write his biography. There had been any number of sycophants throughout his career who had approached him with the idea, but back then, in the bloom of youth and critical success, he had found the very thought repulsive. And yet now it consumed him. It was the only rebuff he could muster against his own frailty, his last remaining defence against Ken's cancer or Ann's dementia – the idea that he had any remaining control over his work, or body, even. He had certainly felt himself less grounded, less present in the here and now since he had passed out in the Lothian Road café. To have it written now seemed suddenly imperative, an urge he could not suppress. Seeing Ken had only reinforced his growing desire to have his story set in stone: fixed, verified and narrated by himself. They were old men, he mused – soon it would be too late, and his past would be exposed to the masses, laid bare for the picking, his life stolen to fill the pages of someone else's success.

No. Better that he shape that narrative. Better that

Barbara be the one to do it. She was a vulture, he thought. Left to her own devices, she would clatter into his past with her ridiculous plastic bangles and plug the gaps, the ambiguities, with her own malicious agenda and fancies. But to collaborate with her – yes, he thought, it would stroke that ego. She would ask difficult questions, but while it was on his terms, she could not go off-script. This was his story. And he was certain she would leap at the chance to write it.

He glanced at the clock above the wall. Ten minutes before she was due to arrive. He drummed his fingers on the stacks of paperwork he had amassed in preparation for their meeting: old reviews, early proofs of his novels with annotated remarks from his editors, letters to Ken. The jewel was at the top of the pile – the typed original of *Victory Lap*. He had carefully added his own notes in the margins two weeks ago with his old fountain pen. He wondered if the ink was too obviously bright, too black, then dismissed the thought as paranoia.

Only Ken knew.

'What are you thinking about?' Sarah was standing in the doorway, a duster in her hand, hair piled on top of her head.

'My imminent demise. Are you wearing dungarees?' he asked, smiling at her. She looked down at herself self-consciously.

'Overalls,' she replied. 'I need them, clearing up your grime.'

He looked down at the desk in surprise, ran a finger along the clean, varnished mahogany. When he looked up, confused, she was grinning.

'You're making fun of me,' he said.

'As is my wont,' she finished for him. She walked over to the desk and idly lifted some of the papers. 'For Barbara?' she asked. He nodded, watching her face. She didn't seem to be surprised or annoyed.

'She'll be here very soon,' he said, glancing anxiously at the clock. But Sarah had spotted the copy of *Victory Lap*, her eyes widening as she lifted the first page.

'You're really going to speak to her about it?'

He studied her face for a moment and wondered at the hurt there. She was in her forties now, small lines beginning to appear across her forehead and at the edges of her eyes. Divorced, of all the ridiculous things his little girl could be.

'Yes,' he said, simply.

Oh, yes, he realised – there was hurt there.

She smoothed the paper back into place and bit her lip. 'Would you like me to sit in while you speak with her?'

He hesitated. She brushed a small tear from her eyelash, and he thought he might hate himself.

'Ken's coming,' he said.

'Good. He'll make sure she behaves herself.'

They laughed a bit at this. She stood and stared at him for a moment, her face composed, eyes a little pink. She nodded again.

'I'm glad you're talking about it to someone,' she said.

He reached over and patted her hand. She gulped, shook her hand free and rubbed at her eyes.

'Sarah,' he said, and then the doorbell rang.

She laughed in a stuttering sort of way. 'Your guests,' she

said, leaving him to stare at the papers on the desk.

You're a bastard, Lewis Carson.

He listened to her trot down the stairs and open the door, the deep bass of Ken's voice overriding the softer tones of Barbara's. She laughed at something Ken said, and Lewis winced.

They appeared in the doorway together several minutes later, her arm linked through Ken's. Lewis, somewhat consternated, wondered for a moment how and when they had become such fast friends before realising that Barbara was supporting him. The walk upstairs had left him breathless, and his gait was laboured – indeed, it was more of a shuffle, really. Barbara caught his eye as she eased Ken into the chair. She looked rather grave, a sharp contrast to her bold outfit.

Her satin blouse was very low-cut and a rather violent shade of turquoise. A large, gaudy necklace rested against her cleavage. He thought about their meeting in the café and decided it might be an act of defiance. Perhaps she wasn't as feeble or stupid as he thought. Good.

'Maybe we could relocate to the ground floor next time?' Barbara said, nodding meaningfully at Ken.

'No need!' Ken asserted, the words carried by a wheeze.

Barbara shrugged and took the chair next to him. An uncomfortable silence followed, and Lewis realised she expected him to take the lead. He was momentarily surprised and made a show of shuffling his papers before clearing his throat and addressing them.

'Thank you both for coming,' he offered, feeling lame.

Now that Barbara was sitting in front of him, her gaze

taking in the room around her, he was anxious. She had the appearance of a Christmas bauble, her blonde hair and colourful shirt a bright, tacky spectacle against the otherwise sombre browns and greens of the study. She smiled at him, aware of his gaze, and it occurred to him that most people found Christmas baubles to be cheery, attractive things.

'So where do you want to start, Lewis?' she asked. She bent down to fish out her dictaphone and pen and paper from her bag. Ken watched her with some interest.

'Right at the beginning,' Lewis said.

Ken's head swivelled round to face him. 'Your bonny Edinburgh childhood?' he snorted, amused.

'No. With *Victory Lap* – right at the beginning.'

He was rewarded by two surprised stares. Recovering quickly, Barbara switched on the recorder and accepted the manuscript Lewis proffered her. Her gaze was greedy as she drank in the first page. Her attention diverted, Lewis took a moment to meet Ken's eye. He looked pallid, and perhaps confused. Lewis tried to somehow telegraph to him that it was fine, but Ken merely sighed and averted his gaze.

'Start from the beginning, then,' Barbara said, flashing him a dazzling smile.

His anxiety dissipated and he decided he had done the right thing. Barbara would remain onside.

'Well, the beginning is difficult to pinpoint,' he said, throwing a quick look at Ken.

'No, it's not,' Ken interjected. 'It started with a girl.'

Barbara grinned, Lewis frowned. He and Ken stared levelly at one another.

'With Ann, of course,' Barbara filled in.

Lewis broke off his mute stare and nodded gratefully.

'Yes,' he said. 'Yes, I suppose you could say things changed when I met Ann.'

'Behind every good man…' Barbara trailed off, a small smile on her lips as she scribbled some notes.

Ken appeared unruffled and smirked at him over Barbara's bent head.

'I'm here to fill in all the gaps he can't remember,' he said to her. 'Lewis always did have his own interpretation of the truth.' Sensing some tension, Barbara's head rose and she stared at them both.

'It's good that you're here,' she said, cautiously. 'You've been alongside Lewis throughout his entire career, and that insight is something I want to harness. But first let's have Lewis tell it as he remembers things.'

Again, she had surprised him. He smiled at her, while Ken nodded perfunctorily. Lewis had evidently underestimated his ire at not being kept in the loop. He wondered if including Ken had been a mistake. He had assumed he would act as an ally in this, keeping him on-track. No matter. Ken could be petulant, but he would hide the truth, to save his own skin if nothing else.

'As I was saying,' he broke the pause, 'I suppose things did change when I met Ann. We met through Ken, actually. He had put together a very small group of writers. He had an eye, I think. Certainly both Ann and I went on to enjoy some success. Arthur…' He trailed off, frowning. It struck him that he had no idea what had become of Arthur. Ken shifted in his seat, his sullenness replaced by an alert interest.

'That's right – Arthur,' he said, smiling to himself. 'He was dreadful.' They shared a bemused grin, and Lewis was glad the tension had resolved itself so easily.

'This would be…Arthur Clarke?' Barbara asked.

They both looked at her in mild surprise.

'I wrote about *Victory Lap* for my Master's thesis,' she said. 'I've done my research.'

'I didn't know that,' Lewis replied, flattered. Her cheeks flushed with pleasure and she leaned forward eagerly.

'Oh, yes. It always fascinated me, how much your writing changed after the first novel. It was the only novel you ever wrote in the first person, the only one featuring a female narrator. Your rejection of it later in your career…' She trailed off, perhaps worried that she had said too much. Reading no anger in his stare, she ploughed on. 'What was it that caused you to create that distance, creatively and personally, from *Victory Lap*?'

Ken was watching him. Lewis scratched at his jaw as though mulling her question over. In reality, he was biding his time lest his rehearsed answer seem unnatural.

'It's an excellent question, and you're certainly not the first person to ask it,' he said, smiling. 'I wrote *Victory Lap* when I was very young. I was in love, I was naïve, unschooled. It brought me great success, and for a while I was purely grateful for it. But with each new book, my reviews would always track back to it: how they compared to one another, favourably or otherwise, and other nonsenses about its *enduring influence*, whatever that was. It seemed that no matter how much hard work or how much sweat I put into a new book, *Victory Lap* would always overshadow it.' He paused, swallowed as he realised he wasn't sure where to go next. 'I resented it – it was a rash idea that held my name hostage to it.'

'A rash idea?'

She was too quick, had pounced on his stumbled phrasing. He cursed himself. It was not what he had meant to say. He cleared his throat and met Ken's eye briefly.

'By which I mean…it was too raw, perhaps? With my later books, I would slavishly plot and plan them, sometimes for many, many months before I started writing. *Victory Lap* was more…rushed. A bit teenaged, if you like. Hot-headed. As I was! I didn't want that short period of my life to define the rest of my career.'

'His poor fans. Not very grateful, eh?' Ken said, nudging Barbara's arm and rolling his eyes.

She did not answer, too busy writing a note to notice.

Again, Lewis met Ken's gaze above her bent head. Ken nodded at him. *Good job*, he seemed to say.

London, 1953

Freddie paced back and forth in his office, a pair of braces swinging loosely against his trouser legs, his hair an erratic mess. Lewis was seated in a chair at the other side of the desk, trying to smooth the wrinkles out of his shirt and resolutely avoiding looking at him.

They were the only remaining members of staff in the office. When the police had left Freddie and he had announced the news, two secretarial staff had broken down in tears, and Nicholas Black had vomited into a waste paper basket, prompting him to send the entire workforce home. Lewis had arrived just over an hour later, ushered through the locked door by an ashen-faced Freddie.

He was quite furious, unable to look at Freddie nor ask him – again – what had happened the night before. He concentrated first on his shirt, then began examining a ragged nail. He thought about his last visit to the office and frowned to himself. His life had become more complicated that day.

He was aware from the flicker of movement in his peripheral vision that Freddie had begun to pause his pacing for brief junctures and appeared to be watching him. He suddenly recalled the way in which he and Cathy would force their childhood secrets from one another – a petty, prolonged game, amplified by malevolent stares. One could never break the silence first: to ask what the secret was would be pleading and pathetic, to reveal it without first lording it over the other, feeble. They would spend seemingly endless hours prowling restlessly around one another, desperate to speak but too proud to break the vow of silence. Cathy was always the first to concede.

He reminded himself that he was no longer a child and forced himself to look up. Freddie stopped pacing and stared back at him, his skin pale and waxy.

'Will you please explain to me what happened last night?' he asked, and he was glad there was no rebuke in his voice.

Freddie exhaled slowly before sitting down and resting his head in his hands. When he spoke, he spoke to the desk.

'She drank an extravagant amount of wine,' he said. 'Spoke endlessly about absolute garbage. I honestly thought we had been worrying for nothing. She didn't mention you at all, seemed perfectly happy to be out and seen with me.'

'And?'

'And then we left the restaurant. I made to leave, and suddenly she seemed very sober. She was…malicious.' He looked up, his eyes red-rimmed. 'Threatened to tell my father, tell everyone.'

'And you left it at that?' Lewis felt how useless the lie was as soon as it left his tongue.

Freddie shook his head. He opened the desk drawer and withdrew a pack of cigarettes. He put two in his mouth and bent his head to light them before handing one to Lewis. His throat felt tight and he didn't want it, but he took it and let it rest idly in his hand.

Freddie took a deep drag before continuing. 'I convinced her to let me walk her back to her flat. Made allusions to making it worth her while.'

'You were going to buy her off?'

'If I had to.' Freddie blew a plume of smoke out the side

of his mouth and looked gravely across the desk at him.

'Lewis, I'm getting married next month,' he said, his tone very even.

Lewis laughed. When Freddie continued to stare at him, his expression tinged with pity, the laugh died in his throat.

'You're getting married next month,' he repeated, and marvelled at how calm he sounded.

Freddie stubbed the cigarette out and leaned back in his chair. He folded one knee over the other, smart white socks appearing in the gap below his trouser leg, and Lewis was reminded horribly of the day he had been promoted.

'Her name is Janine,' Freddie said. 'She's a very nice girl.'

'Well, yes. I can see now why you were so concerned,' Lewis replied lightly, falsely.

'Don't be childish,' Freddie snapped. 'Did you expect us to live out our days in queer bliss? I was engaged long before I met you, and fucking you wasn't going to change that.'

Lewis felt himself blanch, sickened. 'I suppose not,' he said, appalled at the weakness of his voice. For a moment, Freddie appeared chastened. He made as if to stand, but the hateful glare Lewis directed at him made him pause.

'I didn't mean to be so blunt,' he said.

'Tell me about Julie,' Lewis responded, scrubbing his face with his palms.

Freddie stared at him for a moment. 'She wanted too much. More than I could feasibly promise,' he said, his voice low.

'Did you plan it? Did you think about doing it before you got to her flat?'

'No!' His voice was harsh and he jabbed a finger on the

desk. 'She wouldn't… She wouldn't…'

'Wouldn't what, dammit?'

'She wouldn't shut her mouth,' he snarled, spittle landing on the desk between them. He let out a rasping sob. 'I was… livid. I just wanted her to shut up. I didn't… I didn't realise what I'd done until she stopped struggling.'

Lewis stood abruptly. Freddie gaped at him in surprise, his face pale.

'Where are you going?' he asked, frantically.

'Anywhere but here,' Lewis said, and made sure he did not slam the door on his way out.

✳

He found himself walking across the road to the King's Head, unable to face going home. The possibility of meeting Mrs Bell on the stairs was too high, while the thought of his room, messy and stale, seemed too confining.

He entered the pub, bought a bottle of wine and retreated to the darkest corner he could find. He felt calm, serene even.

Freddie was getting married. Freddie was a murderer.

It was a curious thing, to be able to identify the precise moment he stopped loving Freddie. Or at least stopped *falling* in love him. Lewis wasn't quite sure what normal people considered love, or the appropriate length of time to decide one was feeling it. All he knew was that it was gone. Whatever it was that made it near impossible to drag his eyes from Freddie, that made his pulse quicken when he touched him, was gone.

Janine, he mused. He thought briefly of Freddie's hand on a fine, feminine cheek, but it was Julie's face he pictured.

He wasn't sorry that she was dead. It struck him as a horrible truth, truer than anything he had known in his life. A truth that, once formed, he could never un-think, a rank stain he would never be able to rub away. And not only was he not sorry, he was glad.

It always seemed that great shocks in his life brought greater self-awareness. When his mother had died, it had struck him how much he loathed his father. Without her there to bind the two of them together in the illusion of mutual love, his father seemed suddenly a cold, detached man.

And now this. He realised with interest that it wasn't revulsion for Freddie's act he felt, but revulsion for his ill-handling of it, for his unforgiveable loss of control. Freddie's aloofness, his slight cruelty and the aura of power that he had been so maddeningly attracted to had been spoiled by his performance last night and this morning. Freddie wasn't a man, Lewis thought. He was a stupid, snarling child, lashing out at the things he felt threatened by. He had achieved what they needed, but not well.

Lewis permitted himself a moment to consider how he might have dealt with Julie himself. He wouldn't have dined with her in public, for a start. That had been absolute foolishness on Freddie's part, and it was this they had argued so fiercely over on Thursday evening. No. Julie walked home at night. She disdained London buses and chose instead to walk the two miles to her flat, something she discussed at exasperating length in the office. Plenty of opportunity to seek a private moment then, Lewis thought.

He moved to fill his wine glass and was surprised when a young man sat down in the chair opposite him. He thumped his own drink onto the table between them and smiled at Lewis.

'You're a Hobbs man,' he said.

Lewis blinked, taken aback by the insinuation he read there. 'If by which you mean I work there…'

'I know you do! You were here a couple of weeks ago with your colleagues. I'm Gerard Walsh.' The man stuck his hand across the table, beaming.

Lewis took it warily, and they exchanged a brief shake.

Gerard Walsh looked to be about twenty. He had very fair hair and bushy blonde eyebrows, and he made Lewis uncomfortable with his penetrating stare. His eyes were extremely blue, and too bright. Perhaps he was drunk, Lewis thought. His cheeks were certainly quite red, and his demeanour suggested a certain lack of inhibition. He continued to smile inanely at Lewis across the table, and he felt his irritation rising. He chose not to help Walsh out and waited in silence for him to provide an explanation for his intrusion.

'I don't mean to take liberties,' he said, though he looked far from sorry. 'It's just that you never see Hobbs folk in here during the day. It seemed like…oh, I don't know, providence or something that you were here this afternoon.'

'Do you have a manuscript you wish me to look at?' Lewis asked, realising the young man's intent.

Walsh's eyes widened in surprise, but he immediately

ducked down and produced a thick manuscript from his satchel, which he thrust across the table. Lewis became aware of his role in the situation.

'Hold your horses,' he said, smirking. 'I didn't say I wanted to see it.'

The man's face fell, and his already flushed cheeks seemed to darken slightly. Lewis mentally thanked Freddie for the line and leaned back to cross his ankles, maintaining a tense silence.

'I'm sorry – I didn't mean to presume,' Walsh said, terribly embarrassed.

'It's quite alright. But perhaps you could tell me something about the novel before you expect me to devote my evening to reading it.'

Walsh brightened, and for an unpleasant moment Lewis saw himself in the man. It was distasteful, to see oneself so clearly in someone else. But he dismissed the thought. Walsh would have to defer to him. Lewis nodded at him to go ahead.

Gerard Walsh launched into an expansive description of his debut novel. Lewis was not so much fascinated by the proposed content – a turgid satire of some sorts – as he was by Walsh's forceful passion. He spoke at a wild pace, his hands moving as he talked, his eyes bright and intense. At what point had Lewis set aside his own hunger for writing, he wondered? He thought that it might have been around the time he stepped into Freddie Hobbs' office. This rankled. The fool of a man had been quite diverting.

Walsh had paused his monologue to light a cigarette. He

held the packet out to Lewis, who accepted one and sat back.

'Well?' Walsh repeated, and Lewis realised he had not heard the question. 'Will you read my manuscript, Mr Carson?'

That was interesting. He had not told him his name. This sent a flush of pleasure through him. Ann was right – he was someone of importance to writers now. Sought after, even. He savoured the authority he held over the writer for a moment, glanced at the woman by the bar who was watching their exchange with some interest. Another writer, or Walsh's girlfriend, perhaps? He smiled as he realised how his next words would impact the two.

'Come by my office next Monday,' he said, though he had neither the intention nor the authority to pass the book on to the editorial board. Walsh practically leapt from his chair, an unexpected 'Yes!' shouted across to the woman at the bar.

Lewis smiled, pleased with himself. He had quite forgotten about Julie.

Lewis stretched a cramped hand and looked out of the small window above his desk. He had written all night, he realised, taking in the faint whisper of daylight beginning to emerge over the buildings opposite.

He looked over at the bed. Ann was curled on top of his sheets, still in her blouse and skirt. She had kicked her shoes off and taken her hair down, and appeared to be in a deep sleep.

They had quite literally bumped into one another as he left the King's Head, his mood elevated in the wake of Gerard Walsh's enthusiastic gratitude. He wanted to write, he realised. He wanted to put pen to paper and put Gerard Walsh's tripe to shame. When he collided with Ann, about to enter the pub with some brown-haired woman she worked with, his good cheer made her flush, and she seemed delighted by him.

'I'm going home to write,' he told her, grinning. 'It's like there's a frenzy upon me!'

'Quite,' she laughed, her eyes bright. 'I can't wait to read it,' she added, and the idea was upon him.

'Come with me,' he urged, putting his hands unselfconsciously around her waist.

She flushed deeply, and her quiet companion raised an eyebrow in arch misunderstanding. Lewis didn't care. Freddie's absence, which would have nipped and rankled at him only two days prior, now came upon him as an elation. He would write and he would live and Freddie and his Janine could go hang. No Julie, no Freddie – this was better, he decided.

'But you're going to be busy, writing,' Ann said, looking up at him in a sort of happy confusion.

'Yes, and you're my star reader. No one gives me feedback like you do, Ms Barbour. I can bounce my ideas off you as they come to me, and you can cackle at my ineptitude and demand changes. I'll even provide wine and dinner,' he said, gently swaying her body from side to side, as though they were dancing.

She flickered a look at her friend, who merely shrugged, a small smile on her lips.

'Go on,' he cajoled, 'be my muse.'

That had sealed it, he saw. She laughed and nodded, promised to see her friend soon, and they walked back to his flat with their arms linked.

He made them a sort of indoor picnic for dinner – strong cheddar cheese, white bread, some cold cuts of meat and biscuits – and they had drunk an entire bottle of red wine before he had even sat down at his desk. Ann perched on the edge of the bed, and he talked her through the outline. When the scratch of his pen on the paper replaced the bulk of their conversation, she lay back on his bed with a small book of poetry. She would occasionally appear at his side with a pot of tea, though he hadn't noticed her move or heard the kettle on the stove.

He was enthralled by the whole scenario, from the almost fevered pace at which he wrote to Ann's soft smiles and admiration as she lay across the room from him. He studied her for a moment, asleep on the bed. Such long eyelashes. Her mouth was parted slightly, her face flushed pink from the warmth in the room. There was something very innocent about her, he thought. She could be his, if he wanted her to be.

He didn't want to touch her, of course – she was pretty and she adored him, but he didn't want to pin her down the way he'd wanted to with Freddie. She satisfied a different sort of need. He thought that he might enjoy having her around more permanently.

Ann stirred. When she opened her eyes and saw him watching her, she smiled. 'Was I snoring?' she asked.

'Quiet as a mouse,' he said, enjoying the likeness. He stood up and patted the chair. 'Here, have a read at what I've done and I'll make us some tea and toast.'

She stifled a yawn but nodded, touching his arm lightly as they passed one another. He watched her bowed head as he waited for the kettle to boil. She picked up his pen and made some small amendment. A flash of irritation ran through him, but he set it aside quickly. It had poured out of him like a torrent, late into the night. He couldn't expect her to find no faults with it.

He made the tea slowly, wishing to fill as much time as possible while she read so that he didn't have to sit and watch her. When it was ready, he placed a cup by her elbow, and she murmured a quiet 'thank you'. He took her place on the bed and examined the small book of poetry.

'This is Arthur's,' he said, surprised. It was a little cloth thing, its cream pages bound by a thick, expensive-looking thread. Ann looked at it briefly, distracted.

'Mm, yes,' she said, returning her gaze to his manuscript. 'He had it bound for me,' she added.

Lewis frowned. Was there something between Arthur and Ann that he didn't know about? Or was this just a conceit of Arthur's? He opened the little book and read the acknowledgements page. 'To Ann' it read, simply, and he felt himself increasingly irritated. Flicking through the pages to the shortest poem, he read it through with a mild snort.

When he looked up, Ann was watching him, her gaze troubled. He smiled self-consciously, and her expression cleared.

'Lovely little thing,' he said, aiming to sound sincere but hoping she recognised the dismissal.

'I haven't finished this yet,' she said, ignoring him and gesturing at the manuscript. 'You've written so much, and in one night! But what I've read so far… Lewis, it's wonderful.'

She directed a beatific smile at him, and he impulsively leaned over and kissed her cheek. She ducked her head, embarrassed but pleased, and he laughed.

'You really think so? Tell me what you like about it,' he demanded. She looked flustered but smoothed her hand across the manuscript and answered him without reservation.

'It's so raw,' she said, her finger tapping lightly on the page. 'Locke's anger at the world around him is almost palpable. He'll make an excellent villain.'

'Villain?' He frowned at her choice of word and saw her falter.

'He's not your villain?' she asked. 'I'm sorry, I misspoke – I haven't read enough. I'm sure I've made a silly mistake.' She wrung her hands together, her face apologetic.

'No, not at all,' Lewis said, waving away her apology. 'I just hadn't thought of him that way. It's interesting.'

He looked down into his tea, wondering at himself.

Lewis was in the office, staring at his manuscript. Ann had left the flat at 7.30am, harried and explaining that she must go home and change before work. She'd hung awkwardly in the doorway before leaving, seeming to want something from him. But he was distracted and didn't have the energy to decipher her signals. He had left at her back, intending and succeeding to arrive at the office before Freddie.

He stared now at her neat note on the second page.

Will the reader be made privy to the event/tragedy that has made Locke so vicious?

He sighed. Silly girl. Locke was no more vicious than himself. She had confused his sense of the character, and he frowned down at the page. He started at the rap on the door, but relaxed and gestured Ken in upon seeing his ruddy face in the doorway.

'Thanks for coming at such short notice, Ken,' he said.

'Aye, you're fine,' Ken replied, sitting down opposite him and moving to take the manuscript from the desk. 'I was glad you called. So you want to go ahead with Crothers?'

'Yes. But with this manuscript.'

Ken paused, lifted his eyes from the manuscript on the desk and met Lewis's gaze steadily.

'You think this is better?' he asked. Lewis nodded, though he still hadn't read the Watson sample.

'I'm certain of it,' he said.

Ken shrugged, unconvinced, but he pulled the manuscript onto his lap. Lewis pretended to busy himself with paperwork while he read, but he was aware of Ken's small movements, his murmurs and sighs. He occasionally looked up at him from below his lashes, but Ken's expression was inscrutable. He consciously stilled his knee, which he realised had been bouncing beneath the desk.

Ken cleared his throat and put the short manuscript back on the desk between them. 'No,' he said, simply.

Disappointment and self-pity washed over Lewis in a staggering wave. He felt his knee judder again and he snatched the pages back.

'Why not?' he asked, his tone icy.

Ken rolled his eyes. 'Let's not be infantile,' he chided, and Lewis flushed.

'I'm asking for your constructive criticism.'

Ken shrugged, infuriatingly blasé. 'It's not that there's anything wrong with it per se,' he said, his hands outstretched as though he was trying to grasp his words from the air. 'It's just not as good as the text I saw at the library.'

'I can't give you that one.'

Ken's eyebrows rose eloquently towards his hairline. 'Why not?' he asked, sounding somewhat exasperated.

Lewis glared down at the manuscript, the words that *Infinite Eden* belonged to someone else choked in his throat. Envy swelled up from his stomach and threatened to gush from his mouth, a black bile he seemed unable to swallow back. It was unfair, he thought. That dull slattern. This was *his* chance, *his* opportunity. First disparaged by Freddie, now this. The insult stung sharply, and he felt his fists clench on the table.

'Christ, Lewis, I don't know why you're so hell-bent on this one.' Ken gestured dismissively to the manuscript under Lewis's fists. 'It's good. Very good, even. But *Infinite Eden* –'

'Stop, stop, please,' Lewis said, his anger abating.

Ken opened his mouth to reply but was cut off by the door opening behind him.

Goldstein stopped short in the doorway, his eyes on Ken.

Lewis noted that his tie was loose, knotted in an odd, strangled sort of way halfway down his shirt, which was also unbuttoned at the neck.

'Sorry, Carson, didn't realise you had someone in. It's just that the police have cuffed Hobbs and taken him from his office. He's screaming bloody murder.'

Lewis wondered for a moment why Goldstein had come to fetch him specifically. Julie aside, he was quite certain nobody at the office had any reason to suspect his relationship with Hobbs had changed in nature. He glanced at Ken, who was looking at him with some interest. He diverted his eyes and nodded at Goldstein.

'I'll be right there.'

Goldstein bolted from the office, keen to return to whatever spectacle Freddie was causing. Lewis gathered the paperwork from his desk without looking at Ken, his anxiety building. If the police had concluded that Freddie was lying about the circumstances of his and Julie's date, his own role had become problematic. He tried to recall what Freddie had told them.

'Ken, do you remember what time we left the pub? The other night, I mean.'

Ken frowned at him. 'Last orders, surely. It was past ten at the very least.'

Good, Lewis thought. It was a small margin of error, enough to satisfy any questions about his own account. He could have been mistaken. He paused and looked at Ken as innocently as he possibly could.

'Come with me, will you?'

They walked along the third-floor hallway side by side. Heads popped out of doorways, drawn by the increasing commotion from the lobby. Lewis felt his pulse quicken as Freddie's frantic voice carried through the building. They came upon him, legs braced wide apart as if by sheer force of will he could plant himself to the floor, and the two policemen would be unable to move him. A man he did not know trailed behind them, unconcerned.

Freddie's appearance shocked Lewis. His eyes were ringed by stark dark circles, giving him a bruised appearance. He was wearing the same clothes from the day before, crumpled and undone in several places. He saw Lewis and threw himself into a sort of lunge, bracing his legs down against the floor to stop their insistent frog march.

'There, ask him! Ask Carson. He'll tell you I was with him. Carson, tell them!'

The two policemen turned to look at him, and heads in the lobby swivelled in his direction.

It was the 'Carson' that helped Lewis maintain his calm. Something about the impersonal use of his surname seemed to create invisible distance between himself and Freddie, a final, blunt end to what their conversation the day prior had begun. Quite consciously, he realigned his own thoughts. 'Freddie' became 'Hobbs' once more, and Lewis found that he was curiously unperturbed by the scene unfolding in front of him.

One of the policemen looked questioningly at the man who hung at the back. He approached them, sparing Hobbs a dismissive glance.

'Inspector Sheffield,' he introduced himself, shaking Lewis's hand. Ken made to move aside, but Lewis gave him a minute nod. He remained.

'Has there been some sort of development?' Lewis asked, looking briefly at Hobbs before averting his eyes. He hung between the two policemen like a toddler, tired from his silly tantrum. Lewis had to consciously keep an expression of disgust from his face. Sheffield, too, threw Hobbs a look of distaste.

'You're the alibi?' he asked, surprising Lewis.

'I wouldn't say that,' Lewis responded quickly. 'He came to my flat after his dinner with Julie, but I don't know what happened before that. In fact,' he lowered his voice, 'I'm not entirely sure that the timeline the police provided before was quite right. Ken was with me, though, when Hobbs arrived at my flat. He can probably confirm the time more accurately than I could. I was drinking, you see,' he added this with a smile, and felt that it had enough charm.

Ken didn't appear to react to his sudden involvement and nodded at the inspector. Sheffield frowned but took out his pen and notebook and jotted something down.

'Your full name and address?' he asked.

Lewis stared at Hobbs as Ken provided his details. Hobbs' chest was heaving, yet his face was deathly pale. Lewis looked away.

'And what time would you say Mr Hobbs arrived at Mr Carson's home?'

'It could have been any time, I suppose – he was waiting

in the garden, and who knows for how long. We didn't get back till past ten,' Ken said, confident. 'We'd seen in last orders. Me and Lewis, that is. We didn't rush back. We must have met him no earlier than 10.20.'

Sheffield noted this down, satisfied.

'And you would agree this is more accurate than your previous statement suggested, Mr Carson?'

Lewis made a point of smiling ruefully, stuck his hands in his trouser pockets. 'I'm certain Ken's right,' he said. 'I apologise for my confusion yesterday. As I say – the demon drink!'

At this, Sheffield smiled, and Lewis felt relief wash through him. Ken grinned, clearly established as his ally now.

'Thank you, Mr Carson, Mr McHardy. That's actually very useful information. Certainly raises questions regarding Mr Hobbs' timeline.'

He had tucked his pen and notebook back into his pocket, signalled to his officers. As they made to move off, Hobbs seemed to realise the conversation had not gone as he expected. His eyes widened and he struggled wildly against the two policemen.

'Carson! Will you *tell* them? Jesus, Lewis, please!'

Lewis gazed at him regretfully, beginning to enjoy the spectacle somewhat.

'Oh, Sheffield,' Ken's voice held a promise in it, and Lewis tore his gaze from Hobbs to look at him. The inspector turned back, his eyebrow raised. 'I don't know what he's supposed to have done, but he was fair out of sorts when we bumped into him. Upset about something.'

Lewis might have kissed him.

'Upset?'

'Oh, aye. Looked like he'd been through the wars, too. I thought maybe he'd been in a fight, to be honest.'

'Would you agree, Mr Carson?'

Lewis nodded. 'I had quite forgotten, but now that Ken's mentioned it, I do recall he seemed off when he arrived. I did ask if he was alright, but he didn't want to talk about it. We spoke exclusively about work matters.'

'Thank you, Mr Carson, Mr McHardy. I'll be in touch with you both, of course.'

He exited the lobby behind the struggling trio, Hobbs' legs flailing horribly between the two policemen. A muttering rose amongst the staff, and Lewis felt a smile tug at his mouth. When he made towards the stairs, he realised that Ken wasn't alongside him. He paused and looked back. Ken remained in his spot, staring out the door with a flat sort of expression. When he turned and met Lewis's eye, his gaze was troubled.

In the days after Hobbs' arrest, the offices became a virtual battleground. Lewis was careful to sit the fence during the many conversations that took place regarding Hobbs' guilt or innocence. Curiously, it was the men of the office who condemned their boss, while the women generally expressed disbelief. Things climaxed when one of the old guard in accounts declared that Julie had 'probably brought it on herself', a comment for which she received a slap from her younger, scandalised desk partner. Both women were let go, and discussion turned to which woman deserved to be sacked most, if either.

Goldstein was appointed interim Director and did not hide his pleasure over the fact. Dickson easily assumed the role of his second in command, and while the two made a good show of being aggrieved by the situation in an emergency editorial meeting, their glee was palpable.

There were mutterings of redundancies and closure, and the arrival of Hobbs Snr in the office triggered a flurry of new anxieties. The tension was such that Lewis felt his own role in the matter had been largely forgotten. No-one asked him why Hobbs had seemed so sure that he would provide him with an alibi, their minds shifting quickly from Julie's murder to their own job security, a blessing for which Lewis was thankful.

Over the span of those few short days, he thought perhaps things had come good. And then he received a visitor.

Lewis was aware of a strong sense of déjà vu.

He was sitting behind his own desk, the man opposite him occupying the lower seat across from him, which marked the situation as somewhat different. But the natural liberty this seating arrangement would typically offer felt somewhat challenged by the hard stare Charles Hobbs was directing at him.

Frederick Hobbs was very much his father's son, Lewis thought.

Hobbs Snr had let himself into the office without announcing himself, a tall, imperious-looking man with very neat, thinning fair hair. He was wearing what Lewis thought might be an extremely expensive suit. He self-consciously smoothed his own shirt.

'My son has of course been granted bail. My solicitor will call on you tomorrow morning to discuss the conflicting details you have thus far provided the police.'

Lewis felt his jaw clench but he said nothing. Hobbs had not yet deigned to ask him a single question but spoke to him in a tone that indicated a deep level of disdain. Oh, yes. Frederick Hobbs was his father's son.

Hobbs watched him in silence as he withdrew a cigarette from his desk drawer. He was careful that the first plume of smoke was directed far to the left of Hobbs, but the old man's eyes followed its grey journey across the desk with clear irritation. Lewis moved forward to lean on his elbows, the second plume of smoke snaking hazardously towards Hobbs Snr.

'After you have spoken to my solicitor and made clear that your original statement to the police was accurate, you will clear out your desk. I hereby provide notice of termination of your employment with Hobbs. I will arrange for your final salary to be delivered to your home address.'

This took Lewis by surprise.

'May I ask why?'

Charles Hobbs' smile did not reach his eyes. He leaned forward and plucked the cigarette from between Lewis's fingers, stubbing it out in the glass ashtray. Lewis stared at his empty hand before placing it flat on the desk.

'I am not a fool, Mr Carson. Frederick thinks that his secrets are his own, but he is quite mistaken. I know what you are. I know what my son is.'

Hobbs paused, allowing this to register.

'I know,' he repeated. 'And I won't tolerate it. The moment Frederick's lifestyle begins to impact on my business is the moment I put a stop to it. He has already made a hash of his university career. He won't be doing the same to his prospects at Hobbs.'

Lewis swallowed, uncomfortably warm under Hobbs' stare.

'You assume that I will revert to my previous statement – my motivation being what? You have insulted me and taken my job from me. You can't expect a man to feel he owes something to such an aggressor.'

It was a cheap gambit, perhaps, but his only one. If there was some power to be had, he must take it. But Hobbs appeared amused.

'Your motivation being not to cross me. Frederick tells me you're an ambitious man, Mr Carson. If you have any hope of working in this industry, you will ensure that Frederick's stated timeline matches yours.'

For a wild moment he fantasised that he might leap across the desk and choke Hobbs with his bare hands. The thought of Hobbs' pulse battering against his fingertips seemed a wildly pleasurable thing, but of course, he merely sat mute, some leaden thing like misery seeming to weigh him down on the chair.

Hobbs seemed to take his silence as acquiescence. He nodded curtly and stood to leave. 'My solicitor will be here at nine sharp tomorrow, Carson. Do tell him everything he needs.'

The door closed behind him, and Lewis allowed himself a small snarl. He picked up the glass ashtray and lobbed it at the door. It didn't shatter and instead thumped dully against the wood and dropped to the carpet, leaving a grey, ashy mess across the room. The rap on the door that followed made his stomach lurch slightly, as he imagined the satisfaction Hobbs would take from walking back in on the small mess. He was spared the humiliation, for it was a woman.

'What is it?'

She looked behind her, somewhat taken aback and perhaps under the impression that his rudeness was directed at someone else. When she turned back, her face reddening with the confirmation that he was in fact speaking to her, he realised who she was.

'Miss Watson,' he said, frowning. 'I apologise. I had quite forgotten about you.'

He gestured to the seat Hobbs had recently vacated, aware that she was offended. Little matter.

She sidestepped the ashtray and debris, and he realised that she had most certainly heard its feeble assault against the door. As she crossed the room, he noted the dropped hem of her skirt, and a sneer settled on him with comforting familiarity.

She was not petite, but neither was she tall, and when she sat down she was some two or three inches below his eye level. He felt a sort of natural authority realigning, and he was calmer for it. He withdrew the *Infinite Eden* manuscript from his satchel. It was dog-eared from its travels between the office, his flat and the library, which was good because it looked as though he had read it.

He slid it across the desk to her and leaned back in his chair with a smile. She appeared to be holding her breath. He waited.

'Am I correct in assuming that we are the first publishers to see your sample, Miss Watson?'

'Yes, sir.'

He nodded, allowed another silence to stretch between them. He wasn't looking directly at her, but rather at a small catch on the shoulder of her cardigan. She shifted in her seat.

'I do wonder if it would be wise to broaden your enquiries.' His tone was delicate, but she baulked, inferring his meaning clearly. Lewis shifted, feigning discomfort, and he knew that he would enjoy this meeting.

It was after ten o'clock when Lewis finally left the Hobbs office. By the time he arrived at the flat, he had reached an exciting decision: he was going to take it from her.

The idea came to him fully formed, fixed, solid and tangible, an idea which he did not question.

Having finally read the text, he could see why Ken had been so excited by it. It wasn't perfect, by any means. He could already see two or three different narrative strands that he could improve, an entire sub-plot that could be excised to clean up the narrative. He didn't know or care how she might have ended the story herself – he only had a sample to consult – for he could visualise his own ending, and determined it would surpass hers. By the time he was done with it, it would be his and his alone. Fran Watson might have laid the foundations, but he would build the house.

To take *Infinite Eden*, he would need to deal with Watson more adequately than Hobbs had dealt with Julie, and it was with some satisfaction that he concluded he could easily do so. He knew where she lived, for she had included her address on the contact information she left with him some weeks prior. He would act soon, tomorrow at the latest, though only if the circumstances were suitable. He would not approach her in daylight or if she were in company, though he imagined her as a lonely sort of person and decided the latter was unlikely. He would search her flat for a longer sample of *Infinite Eden*. He didn't think she had been lying when she said Hobbs was the only publisher she had approached, which meant he didn't have to fear discovery from some keen-eyed editorial assistant. He worried briefly that she might have told her family about the novel, perhaps even about their meeting, but recalled with a smile that she had told him he was the only soul to whom she had shown the work: 'I wanted a professional opinion, first and foremost,' she had said. 'Lest I embarrass myself.' At that, she had blushed deeply.

And so it was decided.

He would put his hands around her neck and take her life. And then, he would take her work.

He was not sorry. He felt comforted by this new understanding of himself. Perhaps even intoxicated by it. There were people, he reasoned, who were *due* success. People who were ready for it, who had worked hard and were owed it. He was one of those people. Fran Watson was not.

He supposed he would be a villain in Ann's eyes. The thought made him smile.

He did not sleep that night, but lay in a feverish sweat, his plans forming, evolving, solidifying into a clear narrative.

Edinburgh, 1998

Things were coming undone.

Lewis could feel his sense of past and present – and his telling of them – shifting, changing, becoming less precise. The biography project had not been the exercise in control he imagined. Instead, he found himself battling his own shifting memories, Ken's conflicting perspectives, Barbara's keen nose for discrepancy.

He struggled to sleep, an affliction that had not bothered him for many years. He dreamt often about Frederick Hobbs, which was loathsome. When he woke from these dreams, too warm, too regretful, breathless and aroused, he would lie in the dark and remember conversations they had had. It unnerved him that he could remember these conversations with such clarity, that they unseated the sense of disdain he had so long harboured for Freddie. Lewis did not know what he was doing now, only that he had never served any time in prison for Julie Sutherland's death. But his memories of Hobbs as a young man seemed to clutch at him of late, rising up in the darkness with an iron grip.

He even cried one night, in the early hours, when the fact that he had been in love with Freddie became a certainty in his mind. It was with a particular ache that he recalled their conversation that night.

They were on the bed, sleepy but drinking tea and smoking. Freddie was naked, his skin hot, and Lewis admired him.

'Where would we live?'

They were playing a dangerous game, but it was too enticing to abandon. First had been their home, which would be large but tasteful, with a library and a study big enough for them both to work in. Next had been what they would cook. Freddie had lived in Italy for three months after Cambridge and promised delicious, home-cooked *Italiano*. Lewis offered salted porridge and was pleased when Freddie laughed at that.

'We'd live in Paris,' he said.

Freddie snorted. 'Paris?'

'What's wrong with Paris?' Lewis was defensive, but Freddie kissed his shoulder, and when he looked down at him, there was a playful look in his eyes.

'Tell me why you think we should live in Paris,' he said, his tone now very grave but with a hint of mockery lying beneath it.

Lewis felt himself blush. 'I've never been to Europe. Paris is…well, it's romantic and dirty and cheap and expensive all at once. I think it might be an exciting place. Hemingway went there for a reason.'

Freddie laughed, loud and unabashed, and Lewis covered his mouth with his hand, worried that Mrs Bell would hear. His blush deepened, but Freddie was too full of mirth to be angry with him, and Lewis found himself laughing too. He leaned in and kissed Freddie deeply, and for a moment they were quiet.

'You're an innocent,' Freddie said, breaking free and smiling at him. Lewis felt that he ought to be offended but he felt only a flush of pleasure at Freddie's look. 'You're an innocent but you're also ruthless. It makes you terribly enticing, you know.'

This made him frown.

'How can one possibly be both innocent and ruthless at once?'

'You're assuming that men can only be one thing or the other,' Freddie answered, sounding thoughtful. 'That can't be true. Men are many things. I enjoy men who are contradictory, or confused.'

'And which do you think I am?'

There was a pause. Lewis didn't look at Freddie; sometimes he would only reveal the truth when he was almost talking to himself.

'You might not like my answer,' he said.

'Quite possibly. Neither would be flattering, I suppose. If I'm contradictory, that suggests something...calculated? If I'm confused, I'm also naïve, or foolish. But neither would offend me.'

He was lying, but he wanted Freddie to be honest. He would be offended if Freddie thought him foolish. More than offended, he would be angry. But Freddie didn't answer. Instead, he rose smoothly and manoeuvred his body so that Lewis lay trapped beneath him. He smiled, lust in his eyes, and Lewis felt a flash of irritation.

'Have you spoken to Julie yet?'

His question had the effect he wanted. Freddie's smile vanished, and he rolled off Lewis with a sigh.

'No. Must we discuss this again?'

Lewis stared at the ceiling, silent and petulant.

'You're adorable when you're angry, you know.'

'Stop trying to distract me with sex. It's cheap.'

They lay in silence for some time, and after a while Lewis thought Freddie might have fallen asleep. He never slept through an entire night at the flat, and Lewis had a sudden urge to keep him from leaving. He remained still lest his movement disturb the mattress, trying to decide whether it was a vindictive impulse or one borne of need. He decided it might be a mixture of the two and let Freddie sleep on. He must have fallen asleep himself after a time, for when he woke early the next morning, Freddie was gone.

Lying in bed in Edinburgh, Lewis experienced a strange sort of misery recalling this. It seemed now that most of their conversations had ended this way. It was doubly demoralising to realise that not only had he loved Freddie, but he had loved him foolishly.

He had had affairs with other men over the years, but he had never loved – not in the sudden, lurching way he had loved Freddie Hobbs. There was once a young man who had loved him, and he had enjoyed that. It suited his ego well. But his affairs were always short-lived, and always very shallow.

He threw his pillow aside, angry and warm, and lay flat on the mattress, glaring at the wall.

What had he done, allowing Ken and Barbara to trample through his memories? He was choking on the dust of their disturbance, his mind teetering dangerously close to that thing he had carefully, deliberately pushed down over the years.

He did not sleep that night, or the next.

'You'll have seen the news.'

Sarah stepped aside and allowed Barbara to enter the house. She was holding a copy of the *Guardian* and her face was flushed, as though she had run there.

Sarah ushered her into the kitchen and made a hushing gesture – she didn't want her father to hear them. She boiled the kettle in silence and made two cups of black coffee. To Barbara's, she added two sugars. It struck her that she barely knew the woman, yet she knew how she took her coffee. A product of the two months spent delivering trays to the three of them in the study, pretending it didn't bother her that they stopped talking when she entered and started again as soon as she closed the door behind her. Sometimes she would leave the vacuum running at the end of the hallway and creep to the door, pressing her ear against it to see how much she could hear. She was like a child again, she thought.

Well, not quite. Then, in the big writing study in their London house, he'd allowed her to play while he worked. Most days it would be quiet, his pen scratching across the paper (or, latterly, fingers tapping on a keyboard) along with the occasional sound of her fanning out a deck of cards. She would use the sunny square of carpet underneath the window, spending hours at a time teaching herself how to shuffle the deck or playing Solitaire. When she met her ex-husband at university, it was at a student poker night. He had grinned at her as she split and shuffled the deck, fanning it out on the table with expert control.

But some days in the study were less quiet, the days Ken

would visit, or her father would call him on the telephone. When Ken came he brought her sweeties, showed her a card trick, and then they would forget about her. She would stare at her game of Solitaire and pretend she was deep in thought, when really she was listening to the adult conversation. Mostly it was boring. Publishing contracts, book fairs, reviews. Sometimes they spoke in hushed voices about a woman, but never by name and never when her mother might overhear. Sarah sighed. Now she was the excluded one.

Barbara thanked her for the coffee. They sat on the same side of the kitchen table, their shoulders almost touching as they bent over to read the article.

'Jesus,' Sarah whispered. She had seen a variation of the headline on the 6am breakfast news, called to her father to come listen. She realised that he must have known this was coming – 'Carson has thus far declined to comment' – and wondered at the fact that the telephone was not ringing. When Lewis eventually closeted himself in the study, she discovered he had pulled all of the telephone cords from their wall sockets.

Celebrated author accused of plagiarising prize-winning debut novel – 45 years after its publication, evidence emerges that Scottish author Lewis Carson may have stolen the basis for his first novel from an unpublished manuscript.

'Is it true?'

Sarah was surprised. She frowned at Barbara. 'You think I would know?'

Barbara shrugged, turned back to gaze at the paper. Sarah examined the by-line, wondering if she recognised the journalist. Bryony Palmer. Was she a former student, perhaps? From Dad's days as the Creative Writing Fellow at the university? No. The name was unfamiliar.

'This is Ken's work,' Barbara said.

They were both startled by the doorbell. Sarah moved to stand, but Barbara reached out and grabbed her arm.

'Don't,' she said. 'It's the press.'

Sarah sunk back into the chair and felt a flutter of panic as the letterbox rattled. A fist thudded against the door.

'Close the curtains. All of them,' Barbara said.

She obeyed, walking through the ground floor of the house and shutting out the weak morning sunshine, room by room. Barbara dealt with the front of the house, for which she was glad. They met in the hallway, and Sarah noted that Barbara had closed the outer storm doors. She must have had to open the front door to do it. Sarah imagined her squinting against camera flashes, pushing journalists away. She was impressed with this idea.

Her eyes fell on a photograph of the three of them on a ferryboat – her, Mum and Dad – taken when she was teenager.

'Shit. Mum.'

Barbara seemed to understand immediately. She handed Sarah her mobile. 'Call her nurse. Tell her not to answer the phone or the door to anyone.'

By the time she had hung up, Barbara had mercifully removed the batteries from the doorbell's wireless transmitter box, silencing its repetitive sing-song. The thudding on the storm doors continued, though, and they retreated back to the kitchen.

Sarah took a gulp of cooling coffee, her face pinched in distaste.

'Will he speak to me?' Barbara was biting her lip.

Sarah realised that this would impact on her, too. What would the publisher say about the biography now? Would they withdraw from the contract? Ask them to rewrite it?

'I think he owes you that much,' she answered.

They climbed the stairs to the study in silence but for the steady, relentless thuds against the door.

'Will they give up?' Sarah asked.

Barbara sighed. 'Not any time soon.'

She didn't knock before entering the study, and Sarah realised that she was angry. Angrier than she'd ever been in her entire life, angrier even than when she'd discovered Mark's affair.

'Barbara's here,' she said, her voice flat. Her father looked up at her, no expression on his face, and put down the pen he had been writing with. Barbara sat down in her usual chair without speaking, and they stared at one another for a moment.

'Is it true?' she finally asked.

'Yes.'

Sarah's hand fluttered oddly at her side and she clutched at the doorknob to steady herself. She had been angry, yes, but she hadn't truly believed it until he spoke. She was angry that he hadn't warned her, that he hadn't confided in her. But this was worse. She thought absurdly of the night she confronted Mark. His laughing denial had felt like the cruellest slap she'd ever received. And yet this was worse.

Barbara was nodding her head. Sarah saw her regroup, something shifting in her demeanour.

'Tell me everything,' she said.

And so he began.

✳

'So this is the only copy of the original manuscript?' Barbara asked, gripping the copy of *Infinite Eden*.

Lewis nodded. Sarah was sitting on the carpet, her back against the closed door of the study. Somewhere downstairs, someone was rapping on a window.

'This is only about a third of the novel,' Barbara said, looking at the last of the pages.

'I decided not to read the full manuscript, and I never have. I used what you have in your hands as my starting point. The ending is entirely my own.'

'Don't,' Sarah said. He bowed his head. 'Don't try to take credit. None of it is truly yours.'

'Fair enough.'

'Where is the full manuscript, Lewis?'

'I burned it.'

The two women looked at one another, appalled.

'It's lost? We'll never read the real novel?'

That stung. 'I'm sorry.'

At this, Sarah laughed.

'What about the author? Who was F. Watson?'

Barbara was all business. When she spoke to him, her expression was clear, her voice level. He was impressed; she must be terribly angry, but she hid it well. He looked down at the desk, contemplated the newspaper in front of him.

'Just a girl,' he said, finally.

'What was her name, Dad? Fiona, Fanny, Faye – give us something, for God's sake.'

'Alright, alright. Fran. Fran Watson.'

Barbara wrote the name down.

'Sarah, go start up your computer. Search for her name on genealogy sites, things like that. See if she has any living children or relatives.'

Sarah looked as though she might argue, but left the room obediently. Once he was certain she had retreated far enough down the hallway, he met Barbara's eye.

'She did not have any children,' he said.

'Did you know her well, then? Where is she now?'

'Dead.'

She sighed and rubbed at her temple.

'Did she never confront you? Not once, in all these years? I suppose you bought her off.'

He didn't answer, and she rolled her eyes.

'Why hide it from me now, Lewis? The question has been asked. It won't go away just because you don't want to talk about it. That pack downstairs will be asking this and more.'

She was right, he knew.

'Tell me everything,' she said, for the second time.

And he did.

London, 1953

Fran hurried along the street, her heels clacking into the dark and echoing back at her like a yappy dog nipping at her ankles.

She was late, and Helen would be irritable about it. She spared a glance at her watch and cursed under her breath, hastening her pace. It would be another fifteen minutes before she reached the restaurant. Helen was insufferable when she was moody.

She skirted onto the pathway running through the park, wondering for a moment if she should remove her wool coat. She was beginning to sweat uncomfortably, but to remove it seemed an effort. Worse still was the urge to kick off her shoes. She could feel that her toe had pushed through her tights and was rubbing on the inside of her court heels. Damn. Why were all of her clothes so cheap?

She was looking down at her feet when the man stepped into her path, emerging from the shrubbery on her left. She wasn't even aware of him until she bounced off his chest, and she stumbled in surprise. She meant to say that she was sorry, but his foot swiped out suddenly, and she felt her legs buckle beneath her.

They both fell to the ground, and she was confused. He was on top of her, heavy, and she couldn't breathe. *Why couldn't she breathe?* She felt her fingers come up to her throat and was surprised to find his hands wrapped tight around her neck. *Oh. That was why.*

She felt so strange. She wondered if Helen would be wearing the green dress. They were going to have a bottle of red.

As her eyes began to close, she reached out and touched his face. For a moment, she thought she might know him. He jerked away from her touch, but in doing so moved out of the shadow and into the dim light of the streetlamp. *Yes*, she thought. *I know you.*

She tried to speak, – to ask why – but his hands were too tight, the words only a thought, an idea never to be voiced. She found that she was angry. Angry that it hurt and that her feet scrabbled uselessly against the ground, her right shoe falling off so that her stockinged toe turned bloody on the gravel. She wanted to batter him with her fists, scream his name out loud so that someone, anyone, would know what he was doing to her.

But the most infuriating thing of all was that she didn't do any of those things.

Instead, she died.

Acknowledgements

I started writing *The Paper Cell* a long time ago – back in 2012 in fact, when, like the infernal Lewis Carson, I was working as an editorial assistant at a publishing house. I assure you that no fledgling writers were harmed in the process of writing *this* book.

I'd like to start at the beginning by thanking Margaret Hammond, who encouraged a very shy little girl in her writing. Never underestimate the impact of a good teacher!

Lucy Drury and Douglas Skelton provided invaluable feedback on an early draft – many thanks for your time and your good judgement.

To Sara Hunt at Saraband Books – thank you for everything! And to Angie Harms, my editor, who asked all the right questions – I am so grateful.

Finally, my thanks to my friends and family – Mum, Dad, Shane, Laura, Simon, Gillian, Lucy H, Stephen – you've all been so supportive, and it means the world to me.